Footsteps in the Dew

Marsali Taylor

to Marion,

best wishes,

Marsali

This novel first appeared in serial form in the monthly magazine *Shetland Life*.
The edition published by lulu.com, November 2015

IBSN 9781326403706

I'd like to give particular thanks to Gavin Dimmock for designing this wonderful Shetland Noir Limited Edition cover. Only 150 copies have been printed.

Footsteps
in the
Dew

Marsali Taylor

This book is dedicated to
Maxwell Hunter Emmery,
who is as clever, lively and daring as Rannveig's little
brother, Fasti (but much more sensible!)
with love from Granny.

Chapter One

Trial at the Lawting Holm

The causeway looked a hundred ells long, the flagstones stretching through the glinting water to the holm. The Lawman and the officials were already assembled, and the air was bright with their banners. Rannveig knew them all, for she had been coming to the Ting to help sell her father's bowls as long as she could remember. It was their annual fair, held every summer solstice here at the Lawting Holm in the shadow of St Magnus Kirk.

The grass park that sloped down to Tingwall Loch was edged round with stalls, and the centre was filled with people, the craftspeople in green or brown homespun tunics and apron-skirts like her family, the more noble in scarlet, yellow and sky-blue. The community gathered to meet friends and kin from other parts of Shetland, to exchange news, and to watch as justice was dispensed over cases where the local Ting was unable to come to a decision, or where the crime was too grave to be tried within the offender's immediate community.

Rannveig cast a quick glance forward at the low-walled circle, and felt a cold shiver run down her spine, like a shadow on the bright day. She turned her eyes back to the round-towered church. *St Magnus, strengthen me! When I must walk out in front of them all, let me speak clearly.* Her hands clenched on the folds of her apron. Deliberately, she relaxed them, and lifted her head high, looking forwards at the causeway once more.

The lawmen were at the back of the low-walled circle on the island, one man from each herra, including the three from their own island of Unst: Arni of Baliasta, Jakob of Norwick and their nearest landowner, Nikolas of Lund, genial and perspiring in his new red tunic. In front of them were the stones where the officials sat: Rúnólfr the Lawspeaker on the right, and opposite him, Hefnir the Doomster in his black tunic, ready to speak judgement. Eiðr the Lawman stood behind them, for his place was taken in this session by Rögnvaldr the Kirkbuilder himself, Earl of Orkney and Shetland. The

5

Earl's young cousin, Harald Maddadarson, was standing beside him, silent and watchful. The midsummer sun picked out the bright colours: the blue of the loch, the scarlet banners, the green grass, the yellow and red bricks on the tall tower-steeple of St Magnus.

Rannveig's family surrounded her, waiting. Faider's hand was warm on her shoulder. Her oldest sister, Lína, was on her left, corn-gold hair smoothly braided in two long plaits, her blue eyes already swimming with tears. Fasti was running with the other boys, but little Fjörleif clutched Rannveig's hand, her constant prattle silenced. Over at the booth, Káta and Manga stood shoulder to shoulder, their eyes on her; Káta's smile was quenched, and Manga had one arm around her – dear, dependable Manga.

They would call her soon. There was a stir in the crowd behind them, then the tramp of feet. Arni of Baliasta straightened, face dark and set. The Lawman's men were bringing Eilífr for judgement. She caught only a glimpse of his face as they passed: white, as if he'd been kept under close ward for the last month. His dark hair was untidy, and his arms tied. He was setting his feet steadily, as if to hide pain in one leg. His ochre tunic was dirt-stained.

'What have they done to him?' Lína sobbed in her ear.

'He's still alive,' Rannveig retorted. 'They kept Arni's men away from him. Hush!'

In the circle across the causeway, the Lawman stepped forward. His voice carried across the hush. 'You are Eilífr Kadallson of Vinstrick?'

Rannveig dug her nails into her palm. *Answer him clearly, Eilífr, don't let them think you're nervous –*

His voice was soft, but steady enough. 'I am Eilífr Kadallson.'

Now Earl Rögnvaldr rose. He looked across the causeway at the crowd on the field below the church. 'Who accuses the prisoner, and of what?'

Confident footsteps came up from behind them, and a thick-set man in a dark green tunic swung past them and onto the causeway. The sun glinted on his red hair.

Lína gave a soft wail. Her hand clutched Rannveig's arm. 'Eilífr has no chance if they let Lingormr speak first, none! The Lawman and the altingmen will never believe he's innocent.'

'They'll believe it because he is innocent,' Rannveig said stoutly, but she felt her heart sink. Lingormr would worm his way into the confidence of the judges, make them see that night in the house the way he wanted it seen.

His voice rang out. 'So it please you, I, Lingormr of Vigga, accuse him that on the night between Odin's day and Thór's day five weeks ago at the upper house of Underhoull, he murdered Patrekr of Baliasta, son of Arni of Baliasta here present, because of a quarrel over a woman.'

The Earl sat back on his stone, then inclined his head. 'Proceed, Lingormr of Vigga.'

ᚠᚠᚠᚠ

Rannveig had seen only the start of the evening. The children were already abed in the left-hand annexe of the house. Patrekr and his shadow, Lingormr, had arrived just as Mary's star had shone out above the hill.

'A matter of business with your father,' Patrekr had said, brushing past her. She'd served them with mead by herself, shooing Lína out, for she'd heard about Patrekr's ways with a pretty girl. Eilífr had arrived half an hour later, hair brushed and best tunic on, and Faider had insisted he join them. Later, she'd taken them some bread and meat, and they'd seemed friendly enough then. Faider was telling stories of his time in the Norwegian wars, and Patrekr was capping them with the glimpse he'd had, last summer, of the three kings in Nidaros. Eilífr's head had jerked round as she came in, hoping for Lína; Lingormr sat in the corner, pale face shadowed, mouth turned down, listening. He was an odd character, she'd thought, Patrekr's bag boy, you never knew what went on in his head. Now, for instance, he was looking at Patrekr as if he hated him, and sure enough, Patrekr spoke to him as if he was a thrall, not a freeman. He

7

wouldn't have stood for it if Patrekr hadn't been the son of Baliasta, the biggest landowner in the middle herra of Unst.

It was after she and Lína were curled up beside the children, with the bar secure across the inside of the door, that the shouting began.

'There was a quarrel over the girl,' Lingormr's smooth voice told the Lawman. 'The pretty sister. The father had fallen asleep with too much mead, and Patrekr said he'd planned to make an offer for her, but since her father wasn't watching, he'd have her anyway. Eilífr said she was promised to him, and he would wed her in spite of Patrekr and all his high-born kin in Norway, and then they went for each other.'

They had heard the board going over with a crash. Rannveig had leapt up, and run into the house. The men were on the floor when she entered the room. Faider had woken, and was hauling them apart. She'd grabbed Eilífr by the arm, yanked him to his feet and bundled him towards the door. 'Shame on you, do you want the whole island to think my sister's Patrekr's fancy, that you fight over her? Now get home and stay quiet!'

She'd shoved him down the flagstones and towards the hill. 'Come back tomorrow, and you'll see her then.'

Inside, it was quiet again, although she was sorry to see there was no sign of the visitors leaving. Patrekr was pouring himself another glass of mead, a spoiled boy that didn't have to work in the morning. Faider was beginning on his stories again. She laid another peat on the fire and left them to it.

She awoke just after sunrise, and slid out of bed. It was a fine May day, with the sky a blue arch, fretted with wisps of cloud, and the sea dimpled gold. The sand beach where their boats lay was in shadow, but the grassy hill sparkled with morning dew, as if – she smiled at her fancifulness – as if an angel had sprinkled curled shavings of silver over the green blades. There were no footprints to mar it yet, nor traces on the briggistane, so the men must still be asleep.

She'd gone quietly into the room to clear up. Faider was asleep where he'd sat, and Lingorm was curled into his corner, with a blanket over him, and Patrekr was stretched back on the floor with his eyes glaring and his mouth twisted open. For a moment the whole world had stilled, and she'd felt faint. The room swung around her. She had no doubt that he was dead. She couldn't see any signs of a wound, and they'd all thought a seizure must have taken him, but there were threads of sheepskin in his nostrils, Nikolas of Lund told the Ting later, and a sheepskin lying just to hand, as if some strong hand had held it over his face until he smothered.

'I heard nothing,' Lingormr finished, 'and only a coward hand could have killed Patrekr in silence like that. I say Eilífr came back in the night, like a thief, like a murderer, and finished their quarrel.'

Nikolas of Lund nodded encouragement at her across the causeway. Faider's hand tightened on her shoulder. Rannveig took a deep breath. 'He did not,' she called into the silence. 'I wish to speak.'

The Earl looked up and round, eyes searching the crowd for her. She transferred Fjörleif's clutching hand to Lina, and took a step forward, her heart jumping in her throat. She saw the Earl notice her, and lean back to murmur to the Lawman, who beckoned Nikolas forward. She could imagine what he was saying: 'The oldest daughter of Reifr of Underhoull, the clibber worker. His wife died four years ago. She keeps house for him, and looks after the younger ones. A respectable, hard-working girl.'

The Lawman said, 'Approach, Rannveig Márgretsdottir.'

Rannveig walked steadily forward. The stones of the causeway were smooth as their own briggistanes, which had lain dry on the morning Patrekr died.

The Earl rose courteously at her approach. He was of average height, with light chestnut hair. She did not yet dare to look at his face. His tunic was amber velvet, knee length, with a broad band of silk embroidery at hem and cuffs. The linen under it was whiter and finer than any she had ever seen. His breeches were of soft leather, and his boots of gold sealskin, knee-length, fastened with four toggles. Then she raised her eyes. He was handsome, with regular features, and well-opened blue eyes that smiled encouragement. Such command there was in his look, one who took it for granted he was a leader of men, who would expect even the hills to move if he asked it.

'Give us your testimony, grey-eyed maiden.' His voice made a melody of the phrase; she remembered that he was a poet.

'Sir, I was there that evening.' She steadied her voice. 'When the quarrel started I hustled Eilífr out of the house and told him to go home. It was dusk by then, and I watched him go down the hill before I went back into the room. The men were talking, my father and Patrekr of Baliasta, and Lingormr of Vigga. I left them, and returned to bed.'

She fixed her eyes on the Lawman's face, willing him to believe her. 'My lord, when I rose early and came to our door, the grass was thick with dew, smooth and undisturbed. That was how I knew that Patrekr and Lingormr had not gone home. That is also how I know that Eilífr did not return and kill Patrekr. There is only one path to our door, flagged with stones, and the stones were dry. Nobody had come into the house since the dew fell. They would have left wet footprints on the stones, but there were none. Therefore, my lord, the murderer did not come from outside, but was already in the house.' She took a deep breath. 'My father had no quarrel with Patrekr. It was Lingormr of Vigga who grew tired of being treated like a thrall. He took the chance for revenge, when he had Eilífr as a scapegoat.'

The Earl looked around the people behind her, then returned his steady gaze to her face. 'It seems,' he said, 'that we have two suspects now. We must consider this. Stand there, in case there are further questions.'

The midsummer sun was hot on her bare head. She longed to kneel by the loch, plunge her hands into the cold water and lift a long drink to her lips. On the booth field, Manga had retrieved Fasti; Lína had sat down on the grass, and taken Fjörleif in her lap, rocking her. Beside Rannveig, Eilífr stood with his head down, as if he had already given up. 'Courage!' she breathed at him. The men spoke in hushed voices, a steady murmur whose words she could not distinguish, until Arni of Baliasta said scornfully, 'A woman's testimony!'

'Very well, then,' the Earl replied. He made a ceremonious gesture with his hand, and the officials returned to their stones. The Earl

10

beckoned the Doomster over. They had a brief, soft, conversation, then the Doomster came to the centre of the circle. Rannveig felt a tightness in her breast. *St Olav, preserve him —*

'It is the verdict of this court,' the Doomster said, 'that the two accused men, Eilífr of Vinstrick and Lingormr of Vigga, shall be given to the freemen of Shetland here assembled to judge. If Eilífr first touches the steeple of St Magnus Church, his sentence will be retrieved, and Lingormr of Vigga tried in his place. If Lingormr of Vigga is first at the steeple, the sentence on Eilífr stands.'

A run for the steeple! Oh, St Olav grant that she had spoken well enough to convince the men standing in the field to hold Lingormr and let Eilífr run free. She looked at the knots of men against the green grass, brown tunics, green, ochre, moving together to murmur to each other. No, they were stepping back to clear a path for the run. It was to be a trial between the two men. Then she looked on to the last stretch of sward between the booth field and the chapel, and her heart sank. There stood the group of Lingormr's kinsmen. They would never allow Eilífr to pass them. They would hold him, and let Lingormr touch the steeple first, and Eilífr would be led up to the gallows.

Her eyes met Manga's in despair. They looked together at the group of men, already spreading themselves out, arms at the ready. Then Manga bent over Fasti, whispering in his ear. She straightened and nodded at Rannveig. *Don't worry*, the gesture said. Fasti came running down and dragged Fjörleif from Lína's lap. The two children set off up the slope together, handfast, dark head and blonde plaits bright against the green grass, Fasti talking earnestly to his little sister.

The Earl had risen again. Rannveig saw Eilífr brace himself, ready to run. On her other side, Lingormr was bending forward, knees bent. The Earl raised his hand, and it seemed as though the whole valley hushed, the loch, the church, the heather-green Gallow Hill. 'Run!'

The two men took off together, jostling each other through the ring entrance. Eilífr was just ahead, and took the causeway first, but she could see he was working to keep his steps even. He leapt from the last flagstone, Lingormr at his heels, and went on up the green

11

slope. Faider caught Lingormr around the body, was struggling to hold him, and quiet Lína, suddenly bold in Eilífr's defence, grabbed Lingormr's arm. He thrust them both off and went pounding up the slope. Eilífr was still running, but with a step and fall that wrung Rannveig's heart. Then Lingormr's men were in front of him, spread out, and she felt despair jab him as he realised one would catch him whichever way he twisted. She saw them smile as they began to close in.

Then the children came running, Fasti with his confident boy's scamper, Fjörleif's gold plaits and blue skirts flying behind her, straight into the middle of them. The first man stopped, swerved, the second went down. She heard Fasti's breathless 'Sorry!' as he went on to the next, sending him colliding with his fellow, and then Fjörleif was beside them, bumping into them both, falling, and setting up so distracting a wail that the last one was caught by the leg before he noticed Fasti, who was already head down, running, running arrow-straight for Lingormr.

It was a head-on collision, with Fasti's hard little head landing squarely in Lingormr's belly. Lingormr had the breath taken from him with a thump. He shoved Fasti out of his way and stepped on, but it was already too late. Limping badly now, Eilífr stumbled the last steps into the churchyard and fell against the kirk, one hand stretching up to the first ring of yellow stones. 'The steeple!' he gasped.

He was safe. The Earl raised his hand. 'I declare Eilífr Kadallson of Vinstrick innocent of this charge,' he said. He turned his head to Rannveig and smiled. 'You may take your family home.'

Chapter Two

The Watcher in the Broch

There was always one last day of the fair and a night of feasting before the lawmen dispersed. Already the burning site was piled high with heather and driftwood for the solstice fire. The Earl had given a bullock, and two of his vassals were setting up a spit to roast it on.

This evening was different from other solstice nights, for Lingormr had been hanged on the Gallow Hill that afternoon. Rannveig tried not to look upwards, to see the wooden scaffold and the thin figure dangling there, a raven already on his shoulder. She felt the weight of his death heavy upon her, yet what else could she have done? It was better for the guilty to suffer than the innocent. Still, she was glad that his family had withdrawn from the feasting; she could not have borne to meet his mother's eyes.

Faider's stall had done good trade. It wasn't just that their dishes and pots were of good quality, Rannveig thought ruefully. Every man and woman in the place wanted to come and ask her about that night when Patrekr had died. She answered with patience, telling the story over and over, but made sure they bought something too, whether it was plain replacements for breakages or more elaborate platters for the feasting of Winternights. By the time the shadow of St Magnus Kirk had lengthened to touch the hill behind, and the first grey curls of smoke had sidled into the sky, she had stowed away a stock of bartered items, including two good lengths of cloth as exchange against four large cooking pots, some bear grease for Faider's stiff joints, and winter boots for Káta against four polished clibber dishes. Several segments of silver hung in the pocket dangling from her waist. Once they were safely away from the temptations of ale and gaming, she'd give them to Faider for safe-keeping.

Faider had made a little wheeled cart to take to fairs like this, stout enough to hold all their goods, and with a lid for sitting on during boat journeys. Now Rannveig and her sisters worked together to pack away the unsold pots, stowing each carefully in layers of sheep's wool. Káta and Manga worked steadily, but Lína was in a dream half the time, her sky-blue eyes constantly looking around to see if Eilífr was going to come over to them. In the end Rannveig sent her off to look for the two youngest children. Fasti was liable to get into any trouble that offered, and little Fjörleif would follow where her brother led. Rannveig would let them stay up for the feast tonight, but only if they were wrapped up in a blanket at the fireside, in the middle of the family. The ale would be flowing, she had no doubt.

They'd just lifted the lid over the cart and were preparing to tie it with rope when a stranger came over. He was one of the Earl's men, young and broad shouldered, with hair somewhere between blond and red, and fair, level brows. He had a seaman's eyes, Rannveig thought, a blue gaze that seemed to look far beyond her, as if seeing a distant horizon. He bore himself proudly, like a man who knew his own worth. As the Earl had been, he was dressed in a knee-length tunic with a broad band of embroidery at the hem. His breeches were of soft leather, and his boots were knee-height, turned down to show the coloured silk inside. He carried a parcel wrapped in coarse cloth under one arm. He nodded at the younger girls, then turned his gaze to Rannveig. 'You are Rannveig Márgretsdottir, who spoke out at the Ting in front of the Earl?'

She nodded, throat tightening.

'I am Saebjörn, son of Harald Arnisson, the Earl's man.' He held the package out to her. 'The Earl sent this to you.'

It was soft, a parcel of cloth. Rannveig eased the sacking aside to see close-woven linen, the green of summer moss, and finer than any she had ever touched. 'For me?'

Saebjörn nodded. 'I have two messages. The first is this: my liege lord the Earl has taken the young man Eilífr into his service, to come to the court of the three kings with us. He says that this will give time for the family of Lingormr to forget that Eilífr was the winner of the race to the steeple.'

Eilífr to go to Norway! What would Lína say, to have her suitor taken from her again? Yet a voyage in the retinue of Earl Rögnvaldr could make his fortune. Rannveig took a deep breath and tried to speak as formally as this young nobleman. 'Please give your liege lord

16

the Earl our most heartfelt thanks.'

He bowed. There was slience for a moment.

'And the second message?' Rannveig prompted.

'He bids me say this.' His tanned cheek reddened. He shifted his feet, threw up his head and took on a declaiming tone. Behind Rannveig, Káta stifled a giggle.

> *Truly you excel far,*
> *stone-eyed maiden, autumn-tressed,*
> *the girls with hair of Frodi's milling,*
> *with sea-jewelled eyes,*
> *who have not the eagle's courage*
> *to brave the one*
> *who has reddened the greedy eagle's claw.*
> *When I stand in need,*
> *may Grimnir send me*
> *so true a friend.*

He let Rannveig stare at him in silence for a moment, then made a flourishing bow. 'Your servant, maiden. I hope to see you later at the feast.' He turned and strode off.

Rannveig clutched her parcel, heart beating fast. To have a poem made for her by the great Earl! She wished the fair-haired seaman had stayed, so that she could ask him to say it again, so that she could commit these words that were her very own to memory. *Stone-eyed maiden, autumn-tressed...*

'Let us see,' Káta said, laying a gentle hand on her package.

'Oh!' Manga breathed. 'What beautiful cloth. Feel it, Káta. It's like water flowing. Ranka, you'll look like a queen in it.'

Rannveig unfolded her treasure on the cart lid. 'No, there's enough to make an apron skirt for you both, for church Feast days, and for Fjörleif too, if I can cut it carefully.'

'I won't wear it,' Manga declared. 'This is your gift from the Earl, for speaking out in defence of Eilífr. The Earl's man said so.'

'I'm not sure I understood what he said,' Rannnveig confessed.

'Stone-eyed maiden,' Káta quoted, with a mischevious grin.

'He said you were braver than girls with golden hair and blue eyes, and he'd like a friend like you when he needed one,' Manga said.

Káta giggled. 'You can ask the Earl's man to say it to you again, if you happen to run into him at the feast. Then, if you happen to be lying awake, the way Lína does over Eilífr, you can recite it to yourself, and work out the meaning.'

Manga was lifting up the cloth. 'You can wear it this very night. Let him see how beautiful you look! See, you can pin it here, and here.' She gathered one end of the cloth, pinned it to Rannveig's right shoulder, took another gather to her left shoulder, then brought it around her back and pinned again. 'There, with your girdle to hold it up, and your necklace between the brooches. Oh, yes, this is your colour! It makes your hair shine like fresh hazelnuts.'

Rannveig let herself be persuaded. She was glad, later, when they were all seated together on a pile of sheepskins, backs against their cart, mouths and fingers sticky from the fat-dripping meat that had been handed round, for the Earl's man came up again, and asked if she would walk with him. Feeling shy, flattered, heart thumping, she rose, awkward in her new apron-skirt, but did not dare to meet his eyes.

Her father, Reifr, stood up with her. 'No further than the firelight flickers. If you see Eilífr and Lína, bring them back with you. Káta, Manga, go with your sister.'

They followed quietly behind as Saebjörn Haraldsson led her down towards the loch. He didn't speak much, and she was too shy to volunteer. What could a clibber-worker's girl have to say an Earl's man? She knew that Manga would scold her later for being stupid, but their silence was restful, and his arm warm under hers. They stood watching the moon reflected in the loch, and listening to the swans calling to each other. She thought he would have kissed her if it hadn't been for the girls behind them.

At last he smiled, and turned her back towards the dancing flames and smell of roast meat. 'We leave for Norway tomorrow. The Earl only stopped here for the Ting. After that, I do not know. And you, what do you do?'

'We go home.'

'To Unst?' His steps grew slower and slower as the firelight brightened ahead of them. Just before the shifting gold light touched them directly, he paused, and stepped aside to let the younger girls pass before them. It would be now, Rannveig thought, and turned to face him, hesitant and willing together. She'd been kissed before, of course, but not by anyone like this Earl's man. They looked at each other for a moment, eyes searching, then he slid his arms around her waist, warm and strong, his breast against hers, so that she could feel their hearts beating in rhythm, and kissed her, a long, gentle kiss that set her whole body tingling. Then he lifted his head to lean it against her temple. His voice was soft.

'I'm a landless man, a younger son, but the Earl trusts me as his shipmaster, and pays me well. I'm only tied to Orkney through him. When I've made enough from going a-viking, I'd want to settle down and raise a family.' She heard a smile in his voice. 'I'd like a son as courageous as your little brother.'

'You don't have to mend his clothes,' Rannveig said tartly. 'Or wash his little sister's, when she wades through a mire after him. There are times I'd like a little less of the adventuring.'

He laughed at that, and was drawing her to him to kiss once more when Faider loomed out of the firelight over them. Saebjörn bowed, and handed her forward. 'Sir, I hope to meet your daughter again when the Earl returns from Norway.'

'Our door will be open to you,' Faider replied.

ᚠᚠᚠᚠ

She ran the conversation over in her head the next day, huddled in the sheepskin cloak she'd fashioned for herself last winter. Lína was on one side, yawning and dreamy. She and Eilífr had finally reappeared as the fire began to burn down. Rannveig hadn't scolded, but she hoped Lína had listened to her warnings about the way a girl should behave. Káta sat on her other side, and Fjörleif was heavy in her lap, as Nikolas of Lund's twelve-oared trading ship carried them up the west side of Shetland. The wind blew cold on Rannveig's face, and the knarr heeled over under the red and ochre striped sail, the water gurgling along her sides. The sea was summer blue, dimpling and bright in the sun; the land was soft curves of green that ended in red-stone cliffs, guarded by sea-stacks where the white seabirds wheeled and cried. In the prow of the ship, Manga had Fasti by the hand, pointing out the three shelves of the island of Foula, mist-blue on the horizon. Faider dozed at his oar; the men had stayed up later than the women, passing the ale round. He'd taken quarter of an hour to wake this morning, and if she'd been a wife she'd have been tempted to rouse him with a bucket of water. Nikolas stood at the stern, by the steersman, though she could tell he longed to take an oar; for all his children were grown-up, he was a strong, hearty man who never believed anyone else could do something better than he'd do it himself.

The fair wind brought them into the sandy beach at Lund in the early evening. To their left, the new church stood proudly on its hill; to their right, the green Ness of Vinstrick, with the grave of Nikolas's warrior grandfather on the hill. Beyond the ness was their own beach, with the house of Faider's mother, Amma, just above the shore. Their headland was dominated by the circular ruins of the broch, the double-walled stronghold of the old people. The district used the enclosed circle for their own Ting-place each full moon. Beside it was their house, built by Faider's father. The sun glowed on the pale stones that faced the house, and the twin annexes in front of it. Their two cows grazed peacefully in the in-field. Their dog Oskur rose and barked as they approached, then his tail wagged, and he came bounding to meet them.

Amma had made a mutton stew for their homecoming. They ate, then Rannveig chased the children off to bed. At last, she fished the pieces of silver from her pouch and gave them to her father. 'I bartered most of our pots, but these people had nothing I wanted.'

Faider turned them over. They were the normal currency, pieces of a segmented bracelet broken off. 'Well enough. I'll put them in the store. No peeking, mind! What you don't know, you can't tell.'

What she didn't know, Rannveig thought rebelliously, would do them all no good if something happened to Faider. When she went to bed with the others, she didn't undress, but waited until she heard the heavy wooden door eased open and shut again, then rose quietly. It was clear as day outside, and so still that she could hear the waves washing on the beach below. She watched from behind the annexe wall as Faider made his way towards the broch, heavy-footed from ale, and went straight to the tumbled walls of the old chapel. He looked around him, once, twice, then slid around the gable and into the ruin. Rannveig crept forward, listening. There was a click of stone, the sound of digging, then a suck as something was lifted, the soft chink of silver falling. Faider gave a grunt, as if he was lifting something heavy, then she heard earth being shovelled back. Faider would be out again at any minute. She slipped back to the house and waited in the shadow of the wall. Another click of stone, a long pause, then Faider came out from the chapel. She dodged back, heart beating fast. She had seen movement behind him – she was sure of it, movement in the broch, as if someone had risen from the centre of the stone circle. Cautiously, she slid her face out until she could see with one eye. The head was dark against the blue sky – and then, as her father paused, the person ducked down again. Faider gave a long look round, and turned towards the house. She heard his clothing rustle as he came across the grassy field, his footsteps on the flagstones, then the door shutting.

Here was a predicament! If she told Faider she'd been watching, he'd be angry with her for spying, but if someone else had seen where their small store of silver was hidden, it could be taken away that very night, and with it her chances of a husband, for although Eilífr was lost enough in love to marry Lína in her shift, handsome Saebjörn, the Earl's shipmaster, had the right to expect his bride to bring a dowry. Besides ... Her head lifted proudly. She'd contribute to their household. She'd worked hard enough shaping and selling their clibber pots for this silver. If Saebjörn could buy the land, she'd bring

21

cows, sheep and hens to their home. She wasn't going to let a thief take all she'd worked for.

Faider would go to bed now, and sleep heavily. She stole softly around the house and took a long rope from the workshop on the north-east side. She would make all secure for tonight, and risk Faider's anger tomorrow.

Oskur slept by the door of the children's room. Rannveig put a loop of the rope around his leather collar, and began walking towards the chapel, hoping the dog would have the sense to follow quietly. He was a young dog, surprised at this midnight walk, but willing enough. Rannveig tethered him to the lintel of the old chapel, within the shelter of the walls, and patted him. 'Stay, good dog! Good boy, now.'

Oskur was uneasy, head up, sniffing, tail flattened. He looked towards the broch and gave a low growl. 'Quiet,' Rannveig said sharply, and the dog was silent. The watcher was still around, from the dog's reaction, but he wouldn't be able to approach their store now. 'You'll be warm enough here tonight,' Rannveig assured Oskur. 'I'll come back in the morning.' The dog settled under her caressing hand, head up, and Rannveig crept back to bed.

She was woken by a volley of barking, not much later, at the hour when yesterday's sun had fallen below the horizon, leaving a warm glow in the west still, while the first of today's light spread up from the east. Lína sat up beside her, gold hair tousled, eyes alarmed. 'What's wrong? Why's Oskur barking like that?'

Even as she spoke, the dog fell silent. Rannveig's eyes met Lína's, alarmed. Then there was a long howl that made the hairs rise on the back of Rannveig's neck. She caught up her shawl and ran to the chapel.

She stopped in the entrance, dismayed. Oskur was cowering in one corner, ears flattened, eyes showing their whites. When he saw Rannveig, he whined, and crept forward on his belly. Rannveig came forward, speaking soothingly, but Oskur was reluctant to follow her out of the chapel, and when Rannveig coaxed him to the doorway, he cringed away from the broch. Then he threw up his head and gave another long howl.

Rannveig paused, uncertain, then tied Oskur again, and walked forward, until she could see over the chest-high walls into the centre of the broch.

A man lay in the middle of the broch. His ochre cloak was bright against the green grass and grey flags, and from under his head spread out a great pool of crimson blood.

Chapter Three

The Ordeal by Bier-Right

Rannveig backed away from the shape lying so still in the centre of the broch. Her mouth opened, and her breathing was harsh in her throat, but she managed to stop herself from crying out. The children must not see this, with the great pool of blood spreading from under his tunic. His face was turned down, so she could not be certain, but she thought he was a stranger. His ochre cloak was of an unusual colour, dyed in Norway from lichens there, and of a close wool weave. The thong that held the folds of cloth round his neck was in worked horn, and his boots were made of pale gold sealskin, turned back to show sky-blue linings, and far finer than anything that would be worn here in Unst. His clothes reminded her of the dress of Earl Rögnvaldr's men, but the Earl had left for Norway, and his hirds with him. He might have left one of his agents behind, of course, but what would such a man be doing in their broch, at night?

More to the point, who had been with him? The attack that had killed him must have been recent, by the dog's barking. Rannnveig felt a cold shiver down her spine. Was the killer still here, watching her? She looked slowly around, from the hill past their own house. There was nobody astir in the next cottages. The long finger of the Bordastubble Stone pointed skywards. She looked on, to the imposing bulk of Lund, round to the Ness of Vinstrick, and thought she saw movement there, but the light was not quite good enough to be sure. An active person could have run that far in the time it had taken her to leave the house. Amma's beach was deserted. The broch circle hid the hill below her. There could be someone hiding there, but she would leave it to the men to search.

Rannveig released Oskur from the makeshift tether in the ruins of the old chapel. Nobody would try to steal Faider's silver now. The dog crept close to her skirts, whining still.

'Come on, good dog,' Rannveig said. She went swiftly to the house and slipped into the upper annexe. Praise be to St Olav, the younger children had slept through Oskur's barking, and Faider too, it seemed, but Manga was awake, her eyes alarmed. Rannveig laid a finger on her lips, and beckoned. Manga slid from under the sheepskin cover and came out onto the briggistanes, easing the door closed behind her. Below them, the first rays of sunshine dimpled on the sand-clear waters of Lunda Wick.

There was no need to beat about the bush with Manga. She was only nine years old, but clever and dependable, Rannveig's right hand in running their motherless household. 'Manga, as soon as they wake, take the children down to the stream to play. Say we need water.' She picked up the wooden bucket at the door and emptied it on the grass. By the time Fasti had refilled it at the spout, and splashed water over Fjörleif, and she'd retaliated, and they'd pushed each other into the burn, then been scolded and changed into dry clothes, help would have come. 'Don't let them go to the broch. There's a dead man there.' Manga's grey-green eyes went round as pebbles, but she didn't make a sound. Dear Manga! Rannveig leaned forward and hugged her. 'A stranger. You can tell Káta, but don't let the children hear.' Káta was older than Manga, and starting to stand on her dignity. 'Tell her I'd have woken her if you hadn't been awake already. You tell Lína now.' She jerked her chin at the annexe she shared with her eldest sister. 'I'll rouse Faider and send him to Nikolas of Lund.'

Faider wasn't easy to wake, and he had to go and look for himself before he would be persuaded of her tale, but at last he strode off towards Lund. The sun had risen enough to cast the dyke shadows across the in-field when at last she saw a party of men leaving the houses across the hill, and setting out towards Underhoull. Nikolas was in front, his red tunic standing out against the other men's greens and ochres. When they reached the broch, he stretched up to look over the walls, shook his head and came straight to Rannveig, standing guard just in front of the old chapel. His face round face was drawn down in dismay. 'Rannveig, lass, what are you doing among this? If there's sense in this tale of your father's, this is no place for you.' He put a hand on her shoulder. 'Get back into the house, now, and keep the children with you.'

Rannveig smiled. 'They're desperate to see what happened. I'm here to keep them out.'

His son, young Nikolas spoke out. He looked white and shaken, with sweat on his brow, as if he'd never seen a dead man before, but his jaw was firmly set. 'Are you the only one to have gone there this day?'

Rannveig turned to him, surprised. She barely knew young Nikolas, though she had grown up with him; he was quiet, sly sometimes, a shadow of his genial father. He repeated the question: 'Has anyone been in the broch since you found him?'

Rannveig shook her head, then corrected herself. 'No, Faider looked too.'

'And you went only once, and returned?' Young Nikolas looked seriously at her, his blue eyes grave, then turned to his father, eager. 'We can look, Faider, for footprints, for marks to tell me how this man came here, and who with.' He glanced down at Rannveig's feet. 'Your bare feet will not have left many traces.'

Now she was in trouble! If she told all, Faider would know she had followed him to their silver hoard. She chose her words carefully. 'It was the dog barking led me to the broch, and I went only as far as the entrance. Any marks you find inside will be from someone else.'

'Footprints!' Nikolas of Lund said. 'Boy, you have too many notions. But go ahead, look, look, if it pleases you.'

The path ran past the chapel, and then on to the broch entrance. Young Nikolas motioned them to wait while he went ahead of them, bending to touch the grass from time to time. When he came to the place where the burn crossed the path, he gave a grunt of satisfaction, and beckoned them forward. 'See this!'

There, in the muddied earth, was the plain imprint of one foot, a slim-soled, high-quality boot like the one the dead man was wearing, heading in the direction of the broch. Superimposed over it was another, returning, deeper than the first, as if the man was heavier, or was moving in haste. This was a plainer boot, rounder of shape, and creased by wear. Young Nikolas turned to Rannveig. 'Do you have a piece of leather you could cut to this shape?' She nodded. 'Score the wear marks you see here on to it. Do that now, before the marks can alter. Make it the exact size and shape.'

His father snorted. 'And I suppose the lass is to go round the island looking at the soles of men's boots, now, instead of their faces. A fine occupation for a bonny young girl! Come, let's have a look at this dead man, and see if we know who he is. That'll lead us to his killer quicker than your footmarks.'

He led the way forwards, and the others followed. Rannveig looked at the footprint, thinking. Yes, she could copy it easily enough. She slipped back into the house. The children had stopped their play at the burn, and were staring upwards, open-mouthed, but Manga was keeping them down there, while Lína and Káta prepared bread and ale for the men. Lína pushed her gold curls back from her forehead as Rannveig came in, leaving a flour smear. 'Shall I carve up a piece of mutton as well?'

'Mutton, and some of the salt beef.' Rannveig found a scrap of soft leather, a burnt stick to mark it, and her cutting knife. 'They'll be here most of the morning. I just hope they'll take the dead man to the chapel afterwards, and not leave him here for us to lay out.'

She had just put her copy of the footmark into her pocket when the men came out from the broch, carrying the man on a bier improvised from a cloak and four staffs. Nikolas of Lund was leading them, his round face set in worried lines. She rose and stepped out of their way.

Young Nikolas halted beside her. 'You're sure you've never seen him before, Rannveig?'

His voice showed his suspicions. Faider was quick in her defence. 'My daughter is being courted by the Earl Rögnvaldr's man, who saw her at the Ting feast. She would have no need to meet another man at night.'

'Unless to tell him she'd had a better offer,' Nikolas said. 'Yours is the nearest house.'

Faider's face went crimson, and old Nikolas lifted a hand to his shoulder. 'Son, you take too much on yourself. You have no right to speak to the girl like that.'

Rannveig stepped forward to the bier. The man was indeed a

stranger, dressed with the elegance of a court man: the ochre cloak was backed with reindeer skin, the tunic under it of sky-blue linen that matched the lining of his sealskin boots. His ochre cap lay on his breast. His breeches were of soft leather, his belt ornamented with silver. His pouch hung from it, but no knife. The neck of his tunic was crumpled and slightly torn, as if in a struggle, and there was a dark stain visible at the edge of the cap over his heart.

Her gaze edged upwards to his face. No, she had never seen him before, and she would have remembered this harsh, dark face with its long nose, the eyes set slanted below craggy brows, the sneering mouth. An unpleasant bully, who could have a number of enemies. He was beardless, and his hair was cut short, as if from a recent fever.

'He has no keys,' young Nikolas said, 'but we found this around his neck.' He felt in the dead man's tunic and pulled out a pendant on a black thong, a silver hammer. 'It seems he was of the old religion.' His eyes were watching her with a furious contempt that struck her like a blow. 'A good reason for secret meetings, in a family as devoted to the White Christ as yours.'

He had indeed no right to talk to her so, but she was not going to let him anger her. 'I do not know the man,' Rannveig replied calmly, 'and I can answer for Lína also. Where would either of us meet one who has never been seen by our father?' She held her hand out to old Nikolas, palm up. 'Nikolas, this poor man is a stranger to me.'

'And to me,' Faider repeated.

'Let me show you how he died,' young Nikolas said. His hand moved to the cap. His father shouldered forward, angered now.

'Enough, son.' He turned to Faider. 'I have no thought, Reifr, that either of your daughters would be involved with this man, but you can see that his presence here asks for an explanation.'

Faider spread his hands. 'I can only say again that I do not know him either.'

He had watched Faider hiding their takings from the Ting, Rannveig thought. Could he be a common thief? Yet their small hoard of silver, valuable as it was to them, would scarcely buy this man's clothing. Or had the watcher in the broch been the other man, whose boot's likeness she held in her hands, the man who had killed the stranger, then rushed away from his body?

'We will have him laid in the chapel,' Nikolas of Lund said, 'and send out to Norwick and Baliasta that all men there should come and look at him.' He looked around them, and his head went up. His eyes flashed, as if he'd had a sudden idea. 'No, better, we will leave it to the judgement of God. How can we know what quarrels he might have had, when we don't know who he was? We will wash him and clothe him in white linen, so that the least stain of new blood will be clearly seen, and if nobody will own to him, then we will put the men of Unst to the ordeal by bier-right.' He turned to Rannveig again. 'Your skilful fingers are well known. Suppose that this man is not known here, can you carve us a likeness of his face that can be taken to Norway, so that his friends there would know him from it?'

'I'll do my best,' Rannveig said.

Nikolas nodded. 'I see trouble here,' he said, almost to himself. He looked at Faider. 'This is a courtier, no common slave. Whatever he was doing in the broch at night, it was to no good purpose, I'm sure of that.' The men shouldered the bier once more, and Nikolas frowned, and raised his hand to stop them. 'Wait!' He stared for a moment, teeth biting his lower lip. 'Raise the bier again.' He watched the face as it moved upwards. 'Yes, I have seen that face before, I think, but not recently, and not here.' A further, reflective pause, and he nodded. 'When I was at the court of King David, in Scotland. There was a man like this there. Do you remember, Nikolas?'

His son shook his head. 'I was only a boy then. I remember the king, and that is all.'

Rannveig wasn't sure she believed him. If he had no connection to the dead man, then why this sudden hostility towards her, this need to lay his death at her door?

They left the bier in the in-field, beside her covered workshop, and while Lína and Káta served the men with food and drink inside, she took up her knife and went to work once more. She had a broken sinker weight that would serve, hand-sized, made of fine-grained steatite. She knelt beside the dead man, trying to etch his features: the uneven eyes, the heavy jaw, the deep line running from nose to mouth. His ears were low-set; she marked them with the point of her knife. Finished, she looked from the carving in her hand to the still face. Yes, taken with the clothes, his kin would know him.

It was too warm to keep the corpse above ground. The ordeal by bier-right was set for Sunday, after Mass, and Nikolas of Lund sent messengers to the north and south of Unst, requesting that all men should attend, chief, hird, freeborn or thrall. The boats began arriving soon after sunrise. Jakob of Norwick's trading knarr pulled up on the pale sand alongside Nikolas's, and Arni of Baliasta came in his great warship, twenty fathoms long, her dragon prow shining with gold leaf. He himself was dressed in a dark cloak and tunic, mourning for his son Patrekr. Thórfastr of Vigga had asked to be excused, Rannveig heard Nikolas's wife tell her sister. It was his son, Lingormr, who had been condemned and executed for Patrekr's death at the Ting last week. Thórfastr was not yet able to face so large a company, but he had submitted to the ordeal in Nikolas's presence, and his second son, Hafthór, had come.

There was no room in the church for the women as well, so they stood outside while the Mass was said, hearing the priest through the open door. Rannveig could see between the shoulders of the more important women in front of her. There were family connections between them all: Arni's wife and Nikolas's were sisters, and Nikolas's daughter Márgret was married to the son of Jakob of Norwick. The church was dim compared to the bright day outside. The candles of the altar glinted on the gold of Father Jóhann's vestments and the stranger's silver belt, laid with his clothes by the altar. The bier was in the aisle of the church, with the dead man wrapped in white linen, arms folded on his bare breast, and the hands placed in prayer, fingers pointing upwards, as if the dead man was appealing to Heaven. Rannveig could see the raised lips of the slit above his heart, where a knife had struck home. She remembered the man's belt, with only the pouch hanging from it. Nikolas stood by the altar, looking over the men in the church, ready to call them forward one by one.

'We call upon the Lord, the Almighty,' Father Jóhann said, 'to

33

protect the innocent and make known the guilty.'

Nikolas nodded. 'Men of Unst, as your name is called, come forward to lay your hand upon him, and proclaim your innocence.'

Arni of Baliasta was the first to step forward. He laid his right hand on the stranger's bared chest. 'As God is my witness, I, Arni of Baliasta, am innocent of this man's blood.'

The men came forward, one after another. Inside the church and out, silence reigned. All eyes watched the still form in white linen. The wind was warm on Rannveig's face. Immediately in front of her, Nikolas' daughter Geira choked back a sob. Many of the men were uneasy, she saw, taking oath in so solemn a matter, particularly the younger ones like young Nikolas, Eilífr's brother Björn, and Hafthór of Vigga, who all hesitated as they put their hand on the linen, but the corpse bled for none of them.

The women left then, and the stranger was buried in the churchyard, with a wooden cross over him.

Chapter Four

The Sea-Green Bead

Heyannir, hay time, 1150

The amber sun shone on the shorn field, strengthening the hay, sealing the goodness in. Rannveig gathered the sweet-smelling, rustling grass up in armfuls, teased it apart in the air, and let it fall. The grass was wet and warm under her feet. Two more days of this sunshine, and they would be able to gather the hay into cols. She worked her way to the end of the row, straightened and looked around her with satisfaction. Another week would see the bere ripe; already it was golden, rippling like a sunset-coloured sea in the breeze between the two green strips of pease. It had been a good growing summer, with the right balance of rain and sunshine. The cows, grazing peaceably on their tethers, had regained all the weight they'd lost over the winter. One had had a bull calf, and one a heifer – a calf to slaughter, a calf to keep. There was plenty of milk, and she and her sisters had been kept busy making butter and cheese. The pig that ran round the infield had grown fat on scraps, and birthed six piglets. Faider and Fasti had taken the boat out on the long, still summer evenings, when the sky arched blue and light over the green hills and softly-fretted water, and brought back heavy grey cod, snout-nosed brown ollicks, and mackerel, writhing in their silver, green and black stripes, to eat fresh, and to salt away or sun-dry. Between children and dog, fifteen rabbits had been caught in the hayfield as it was scythed, enough to make a big pot of rabbit stew, and skins to line a cloak for each of the younger ones. St Olav be praised, they would live comfortably this winter.

They were not the only ones busy in the hayfield. In every house she could see, figures were moving among the green-combed fields: to her right, over the hill, at Baila, they were turning the hay; to her left, Olav of Bordastubble and his wife Kitta were starting to gather it into cols, and over in the cluster of houses around Lund, a dozen dark figures were gleaning the last wisps from the sweep of shorn grass between the houses and the beach. Across the dancing water, the brown hills of Yell were starting to be tinged pink with the first heather flowers.

It was a month since the stranger's body had been found in the broch circle, but they still had no idea who he was. Nikolas of Lund had kept his clothes and the likeness Rannveig had carved, and showed them to his visitors, but nobody had recognised him. The thought had stayed in her mind, like a grumbling tooth. Somebody must have known him, somebody that he'd come here to meet. Not Faider or Lína, so it was not Underhoull he was seeking. Her gaze lingered on the broch, only five hundred ells from their house. Either his business was so secret that he didn't dare be seen by the women and children of the household, or he was meeting someone other than the master of the house. She considered that for a moment, and decided that it was good reasoning, but took her no further forward. Jodis of Baila, Olav of Bordastubble, and Nikolas of Lund were the landowners here, but she couldn't think of any reason for them to be meeting a stranger at night, away from their houses. No, a son of the household was more likely; that pointed squarely to Young Nikolas, for Jodis had no son, and Olav's were grown men who'd moved to their own crofts. Or he could be meeting a manservant who was supplying him with information about what went on within the household – but why should the courtly stranger be interested in their small concerns? Nikolas of Lund was important in Unst, but nobody compared to a lord like Earl Rögnvaldr. As for the broch, well, near as it was to Underhoull, she supposed it was the only place within the area where you could have a secret meeting, under cover of the walls. During the light nights of summer, two people out on the open hill would be plain to the eye, whereas someone from Lund or Baila could slip unobserved along the beach and up to the broch.

She had not been able to look for the boot whose print she had copied, for everybody was still going barefoot. Only travellers like the stranger wore boots. Thinking like that led her to wonder why the follower whose step she had copied had worn shoes at all. It might have been to avoid stubbing his feet on stones in the dimmed light, or perhaps to try and match the stranger's courtly dress. A young man who cared about his status, and did not want to feel at a disadvantage?

The water danced before her, and reminded her of a question nobody had asked. How had the courtly stranger arrived here? Nobody, it seemed, had seen him walking around Unst, so he must have been set off from a knarr, or arrived in his own smaller boat. Amma would have seen a strange boat nosing into her bay, where Grandfaider had created two noosts for drawing the boats into over the winter months. Rannveig paused in her thoughts, frowning, and then remembered the geo on the other side of the broch headland. It was steep and rocky, but she thought you could bring a boat in unseen. She would look later, not that there would be any traces now of a boat from a month ago. She brushed the sweat from her brow with a hand, and bent back to her task.

They stopped as the sun rose to its highest, and took a moment to make themselves respectable, untucking their kilted skirts from their girdles to hide their bare legs once more, and brushing off the hayseeds. Káta had gone in half an hour ago to prepare oatcakes and blaand. 'I'll call Faider as I pass,' Rannveig said.

Faider was busy carving bowls, large rounded platters for the Winternights feasting. As Rannveig approached the open booth on the hill side of the house, the chipping noises stopped, and she heard a splash as he rinsed the bowl. When she looked in, Faider was holding the platter in his hands, admiring it. The half-egg shape of rippled stone gleamed in his hands, sea-green and white, flattened underneath so that it could be set down.

Faider looked up quickly as she came in, and laid the platter aside. 'Time to eat at last?'

Rannveig nodded. 'That's a bonny one.'

'Good enough. I wanted to use that offcut that wasn't quite oval, so I made it egg-shaped.' He rose, slowly, grimacing, and Rannveig looked at him with concern. 'My joints are hurting. I'll rub them with that grease you got at the Ting.' He looked at her a moment, rubbing on hand round his chin, eyes looking at her then flicking away again, as if he was wanting to say something. Rannveig frowned. He'd been quiet of late, as if he was worried about something. He took a breath now and turned away from her, speaking out to the bright day.

'Rannveig, lass, you've not been interfering with where I bury the silver, have you?'

She remembered that midnight journey to put the dog on guard, the stealthy head looking over the wall. 'No, Faider.' Alarm caught at her throat. 'Why, there's nothing wrong, is there?'

Faider turned back to her, brows drawn together. His eyes were puzzled. 'And you don't think one of your sisters would have touched it?'

Rannveig shook her head. 'We none of us know where it is. You know that, Faider.'

'Nor you do.' He spread his hands. 'Still, it's strange. You don't think the children might have found it, and be playing with the silver?'

'Not without telling us.'

'No, no.' He straightened his back and took a step out into the infield. Rannveig caught his arm.

'Faider, what's happened?'

He shook his head. 'I'm not sure.' His hand came over hers. 'You're a good girl, Ranka, the very look of my dear Márgret, and with as good a head on your shoulders. I've moved the silver to a new place.' He nodded towards the infield dyke, and paused to look around him. His lips came so close to her ear that she could feel them move, in the warmth of his breath. 'That white stone, there, seven paces up from the corner. It's buried there, on the other side of the wall.' He nodded. 'Now there's one more who knows where it is, should something happen to me.'

'St Olav forbid! But what's wrong, Faider?'

He spread his hands. 'Some went missing. I thought I'd misremembered, but when I looked more closely, there was a half-bracelet that wasn't there, and I was sure there were fewer coins too. That was not long after the stranger died.'

'Part of it?' Rannveig said. 'A strange thief, to take only part.'

'That's what I thought. And it wasn't the stranger, for there was no silver found on him, and just as well, for how could I ever have proved it was mine? So I thought I'd move what was left, only between those orders and the harvest there was never time. But then I

40

looked again, two weeks later, and it had been replaced. The half-bracelet, the coins. It was all as it was.'

Rannveig stared at him. 'Someone took some, then replaced it.'

'So it seems.'

'But why would anyone do that?'

Faider shrugged.

'Maybe the stranger took it, and someone else replaced it? But why not take all?'

'Anyway,' Faider said, shrugging it off, 'it's safe now. The children are in the broch. Are you going to call them?'

Rannveig frowned over it as she walked to the broch. To take some, not all, and then return it ... she couldn't make sense of it.

Fasti and Fjörleif had helped in the hayfield until they'd got bored, and Rannveig had sent them off to play, with Oskur to guard them, or at least give the alarm if one of them fell into the sea, or got stuck in a mire. She could hear laughter floating out of the broch. The dog didn't like going in there now, and lay outside the circle, nose on paws, waiting for them to come out again. Rannveig cupped her hands around her mouth. 'Fasti! Fjörleif! Time to eat.'

There was no answer. She remembered from her own childhood play how the thick broch walls deadened sound. Sighing, she walked over to the doorway. Oskar rose, wagging his tail. From inside the broch, she heard Fasti's voice.

'Now I strike you with my dagger,' he shrilled, 'and you fall dead, and I run away in my boat.'

'Like this!' Fjörleif replied gleefully. 'Ouch!'

Rannveig came around the lintel and looked in. Fasti was creeping up behind Fjörleif, an imaginary dagger raised to strike. Fjörleif was at the side of the broch, rubbing her elbow, as if she had struck it on the stones as she fell. Then she was distracted by something. She reached down, chubby fingers burrowing among the grass. 'Look what I've found!'

Fasti kept his imaginary dagger raised. 'It's only a bead.'

'It's pretty,' Fjörleif insisted. 'Look, it's green.' She rubbed it on the grass to clean it. 'It sparkles, too. I'll ask Rannveig for a thong,

41

and wear it between my brooches, the way she and Lína do.' She parted the grass again. 'And another one, a wooden one, look! Someone must have broken a necklace here.' She lifted her head and saw Rannveig. 'Look, Ranka, look what I've found!'

She ran over and pressed the bead into Rannveig's hand. It was smooth and heavy, cold in her palm. Rannveig lifted her hand to look at it closely. It was spun glass, made by a skilled hand, whorled round and round, and with a silvery sparkle within it. Of course a woman might have broken her necklace at any time, but she would have searched for a bead like this – unless it had been too dark to see, or unless a barking dog had frightened her away. Rannveig remembered the way the footstep had been deeper at the toe, as if the person was hurrying.

The corpse of the stranger had not bled for the touch of any of the men. Was that, she wondered, turning the sea-green bead in her hand, because it wasn't a man who'd stabbed him, but a woman?

ᛏᛏᛏᛏᛏ

Haustblót, mid-October, 1150.

The turning point between summer and winter was haustblót, the great harvest feast, held three weeks after the autumn equinox, as the dark ate away at the daylight, and the hills turned from their royal purple to rusted pink. On the lower ground, the marsh grass darkened to olive, and the bog asphodel made patches of burnt orange among the bleaching grasses. The wild geese creaked overhead, dark wings spread against the pale sky.

In Amma's day haustblót had been dedicated to the goddess Freya, but now they carried sheaves of bere and bowls of pease down to the church and celebrated the Lord's bounty there. After that a great fire was lit, down on Lund beach, and the community feasted on the first beast to be slaughtered, a bullock given by Nikolas of Lund.

42

Little Fjörleif wore the bead she had found with pride, the centrepiece of her strand of clibber beads that Manga had carved from offcuts. In the glinting firelight, Rannveig looked around her at the necklaces all the women had, strung from shoulder to shoulder between the brooches that pinned their apron-skirts. Most of them were like her own, painted wood spaced out by polished shells. Only the landowners' women would have glass. Jodis of Baila had no sons, but he had two daughters who might have worn such a bead. Rannveig looked at each of them in turn, as she chatted her way around the flickering circle, the fire hot on her cheeks. Maeva's strand was coloured wools plaited with smooth, black beads, and Hildr's were smooth white quartz.

There were many women in Nikolas of Lund's household. Rannveig moved on, and thanked his wife, Kristin Arnisdottir, aunt to Patrekr who had died in their house at midsummer, for the bullock. 'It's been a good harvest, God be thanked.'

'Good indeed,' Kristin agreed. She wore a necklace of glass beads, arranged in pairs from a larger central one, but it was hard to make out colours in the flickering orange light. There could be green among them. Rannveig decided to ask more.

'Your husband never got a name for the stranger, who died at the broch?'

Kristin started. 'The dead man? No, we know nothing.' Her voice was steady, but her hands clasped and unclasped again in her lap.

'It was strange,' Rannveig persisted, 'how he came to be there. Nikolas never found any trace of a boat?'

Kristin shook her head, and moistened her lips before she spoke. 'Not that he mentioned. Perhaps he came with the person who killed him. That would be far more likely.' Her face flushed, and she spoke vehemently. 'An outsider who brought him here, and they quarrelled. They could have quarrelled on the boat, even, and he decided to leave the body here, and sail off, so that the murder could never be brought home to him. Then the dead man's kin couldn't claim blood money.'

'Perhaps,' Rannveig agreed. She tried to look Kristin in the face, but the older woman dropped her eyes. 'Yes, that seems likely.' She spread her hands. 'Well, God will reveal all in his own good time.'

A look of pain flashed across Kristin's face. 'Yes,' she agreed, in a low voice, 'the secrets of all hearts will be revealed on the last day.' She rose, shaking out her skirts. 'Excuse me, Rannveig. I must check the women know what to serve next.'

She walked quickly away, catching the arm of her youngest daughter, Geira, as she passed, and drawing her out of the circle of firelight. Rannveig gazed after her, thoughtful. The explanation Kristin had been so keen to convince her of didn't seem likely. If the quarrel had been on the boat, why carry a heavy body up to the broch, when it would be so much easier just to drop it overboard?

Perhaps he came with the person who killed him. Rannveig's eyes widened. *The person.* Anyone else, she was sure, would naturally have said 'the man who killed him.' Kristin's uneasiness, combined with that choice of words, suggested she knew more than she wanted to admit, even to herself: *the secrets of all hearts will be revealed.*

Maria, the wife of young Nikolas, was standing beside her. Now she turned to Rannveig. 'Is Kristin well? She seemed to leave in a hurry.'

'She wanted to check on the serving maids.'

Maria snorted. 'As if they didn't know their work well enough, from the way she chases them day and night.' She smiled at Rannveig, showing both dimples in her round cheeks. 'You're fortunate, to have a household of your own running.' She held up one pretty, plump hand. 'Oh, I know, your father is in charge, but never tell me you don't organise things as you like, and get your sisters to do things your way.'

Rannveig laughed ruefully. 'I do my best.'

'I knew it.' Maria pouted. 'I can't move so much as a platter without Kristin on my back. "That doesn't go there," she says, or "I find this is the best place to put that." Then she puts it back, leaving me feeling like a silly girl. As for Geira, the girl is in a dream half the time, sulking over being kept at home – and why they need still to keep her at home now I'm there, I don't know. Probably because Kristin has trained her to be as unyielding as herself.'

There were flecks of silver in her glass beads, which sparked back the light from the fire. 'Doesn't Nikolas take your part?'

'Which Nikolas?' The girl laughed sharply, a sound with no joy in it. 'Older Nikolas lets his wife lead him by the nose, like a tame bear, and young Nikolas is too busy making merry with the other young men of the place to think about paying attention to his wife. Why should he? He's got his sons – ' Her voice softened, then hardened again. 'A daughter next perhaps, but as long as there's food on the table and beer in the funnels, why should he care if a woman's happy?'

She turned away with a choking sound, and snatched a piece of meat from the platter. Rannveig remembered the way Nikolas had sneered at her over the stranger's body, and was sorry for Maria. She didn't want to see what her imagination showed her, the bored, neglected wife slipping on her husband's boots to walk swiftly in the shadows to the broch, where she planned to meet her lover, perhaps a suitor from the days when she'd been young and free in Norway, before the older Nikolas had traded for a bride for his son...

The colours of her beads were hard to see in the firelight, but Fjörleif's green bead had also been flecked with silver.

Chapter Five

Discoveries at Winternights

Haustmanudur was followed by the first month of winter, Gormanudur, the slaughter month. Rannveig's family had the bull calf to kill, and thirteen of the lambs had been male too, so now the rafters were hung with joints drying in the peat smoke, and there were two full barrels of salted meat in the lower end of the longhouse, and one of fish, along with the hay, packed tightly into the end of the space. They'd gathered the straw and taken it to the byre, ready from when the cows had to be brought indoors – not long now, for the next month would be Frermanudur, the frost month, although here in Shetland, in the middle of the sea, their winters were milder than Amma's tales of deep snow in the mountains of Norway. The nights were dark now. Rannveig paused on the briggistanc to look up at the stars. The first to come out was the one her mother had called Mary's star, though Amma said it was Freya's, and then the square shape of Odin's wagon, pointing to 'the Star', the star of sailors. She wondered where Saebjörn was now, and if he still thought of her.

The Earl should be returning to his Hall in Orkney soon, for the three-day celebration that the old folk called Winternights was the end of summer commerce, the end of journeying. Márgret of Vinstrick was expecting her son home any day now, she'd told Rannveig at Haustblót, and then they'd have a word with her father about a dowry for Lína, for her late husband's son wouldn't consider a girl without goods and gear, no matter how blue her eyes or golden her hair. Remembering how Maria had railed against Kristin of Lund, Rannveig was sorely tempted to tell her that Lína's family would only consider it when Márgret stepped aside for her son's bride, but refrained, for Lína's sake. The girl was anxious enough about Eilífr without beginning a feud with his mother. She hoped Eilífr would make sure his bride was respected in her own household.

The thought of Eilífr reminded her of the first death here, of Patrekr of Baliasta. She was still sure, on the evidence of the unbroken dew, that nobody else had gone into the room, so Lingormr of Vigga had to have been guilty, except that it was a strange coincidence to have two deaths by violence in this little community. She couldn't see any way in which they could have been linked; Patrekr had died in the girls' month, a full moon's journey before the stranger, and Arni of Baliasta had taken the ordeal by bier-right in front of Nikolas of Lund. If he had known the stranger, he would have spoken out. No, she could not see a connection.

Now that the cold had come, and they were all wearing shoes again, Rannveig watched for the boot whose pattern she had taken. She knew it by heart, and a glance at an outstretched foot was sufficient to tell her that this was not the one. She had learned more about the wearer in comparing the soles: a younger person, with a slim foot. Watching the ordeal by bier-right in the chapel, she'd noticed that the younger men were more apprehensive: young Nikolas, Eilífr's brother Björn, and Hafthór of Vigga, Lingormr's brother. Each of them had hesitated before the dead man, as if afraid that blood would flower on the snow-white linen to accuse him of his death. After the hesitation, Nikolas had given his name and laid his hand with a defiant swagger, and a glance back at the women in the doorway. Björn had followed him, looking apprehensively up at the cross above the altar, and Hafthór had stepped forward, footsteps heavy on the earthen floor, and touched the man's brow in a gesture of reverence before laying his hand on his breast. He had kept his hand on the white shroud for longest, looking into the dead man's face, as if he was repeating a vow. Yet Thórfastr of Vigga too had seen the man, and declared that he did not know him. How could a son who was still living at home meet a man his father had never seen?

Rannveig shook her head, brushing the thoughts away. She had enough to be doing without dwelling on a stranger's death. Nikolas of Lund had taken over enquiries about him; that should be enough for her.

Although they were Christians, as King Olav had decreed some hundred years since, and his descendent, the holy St Olav of living memory, had re-affirmed, some in the isles kept the pagan ways still, and each night of the old festival of Winternights was celebrated at a different house: Jakob of Norwick's first, then Arni of Baliasta, then over to Underhoull. That had been a flurry of baking, interrupted by going down to the church for the solemn mass of All Saints' Day. After it, all the families of their neighbourhood came up to Underhoull, and squashed into two long lines along the walls of their biggest room, with Rannveig and her sisters scurrying from one to the other, serving ale and passing out meat, cheese and bread. The older men were here, Nikolas of Lund, Arni of Baliasta and Jakob of Norwick, clapping Faider on the back and asking how he'd got on in the fishing season. Of the younger men, only Jakob's son came with his father, and Björn of Vinstrick trailed in his mother's wake. Lína hurried forward to serve them, and was given a frosty welcome. Old battleaxe, Rannveig thought, trying to bully Lína into submission before the betrothal was even announced. Thórfastr of Vigga and his son, Hafthór, did not come, but Rannveig had not expected them to. She was sorry for the breach between the families, as Thórfastr was a kindly man, a roaring Viking of the old style, who had shouted his indifference to the loss of a wife to Faider even as he'd pressed a length of dress-cloth and a knitted shawl into her hands, murmuring, as if he wanted to disown the kindness, 'My wife sent you this, for the little ones.'

'Your husband is well?' she asked Maria, as she handed around the platters of bread.

Maria laughed shortly. 'He had business elsewhere. His father is not best pleased, I can tell you, such a good server of the White Christ as he is.' Her smile mocked. 'As we all are, I am sure.'

Rannveig had not thought of that. Did young Nikolas hold to the old ways still, the old gods? She saw his hand again, pulling the black thong and silver hammer from around the dead man's neck, and heard his voice, sneering: *A good reason for secret meetings, in a family as devoted to the White Christ as yours.* He had claimed not to know the dead man, had laid his hand on him defiantly. Were they linked in some way connected with the old gods? Was there, even now, in spite of the decrees of St Olav, a meeting of the worshippers of Thór here in Unst, this Winternight?

ᚠᚠᚠᚠ

The November wind howled around the great feasting hall in Nidaros. Inside, the fire blazed from logs piled in the hearth, and winked scarlet on the crowns of the three kings, surrounded by their nobles at the top table on the dais. Earl Rögnvaldr was among them, leaning his chestnut head to his neighbour, and improvising a complimentary poem. The noble women went round with the ceremonial cup: King Eystein's wife, King Sigurd's sister and the dowager Queen Ingirid for her son, King Inge. Each served her man's followers first, then the others at that table. After that, the feast was brought: platters of beef, pork, and wild goose, boiled in a sauce to be mopped up with the round flatbread. There were chunks of fish speared on wooden skewers, and boards of yellow cheese. Brass cauldrons of ale flavoured with juniper berries stood round the hall, for each man to help himself.

Tonight was the last evening of the feast of Winternights. Outside, as for the preceeding nights, the town was rowdy with carnival, masked guizers going from house to house, and music striking up in the streets. The cow-horn pipes were too soft to be heard indoors, but every so often the trumpet note of the lur rang into the hall. Indoors, the red-faced men roared compliments at the serving maids, and clashed their glass drinking funnels together. Eilífr glanced at Saebjörn, uneasy. He'd seen hard drinking at the Ting gatherings, but nothing like these rowdy men in this great hall, whose axes and broadswords lay ready to be used at a glance taken amiss.

Eilífr was well down the table, as his birth dictated, a smallholder from distant Shetland. He stared up the length of the hall at the kings, storing up the details of their appearance. What tales he would have to tell when he got home!

King Eystein was the oldest, in his mid-twenties, of middle-height, dark of hair and complexion, and dark of nature too, Eilífr had been told. 'Walk warily round him,' Saebjörn had said. There were only five years between them, but Saebjörn seemed much older to Eilífr, and already well-travelled. He had smiled as Eilífr stared open-mouthed at the sprawl of houses cradled in the loop of the river Nid, and the ships jostling for space along the banks. The town was dominated by the cathedral, begun a century ago by the first King Olav and now dedicated to his greater namesake, St Olav, whose bones lay in a silver reliquary on the altar. The stone walls towered up from the ground, with helmeted gargoyles spouting water, or making faces at the passers below them.

The situation in Nidaros was tense. The oldest of the kings, King Eystein, was also the newest, for he'd been brought up in Scotland as a landless bastard, and come to Norway just eight years back, to claim his birthright as the late King Harald's son.

'He's prudent and able, as befits a king,' Saebjörn had said one day, as they were returning through the narrow streets to the bishop's lodge, where Earl Rögnvaldr and his men were billeted, 'but he won't lay out a silver piece that he doesn't have to, and he's narrow-minded in his ideas – too narrow-minded, so that the dowager Queen Ingirid and the counsellors don't listen to him any more, although they say he's also willing to listen to reason.' Saebjörn looked over his shoulder, and leaned closer. 'He's been heard to speak against the queen, and it's common knowledge that he and her son, Inge, don't get on. Inge believes that the other two are planning to de-throne him.'

King Inge was sitting in the middle of the high dais, a half-brother on each side, a gold circlet on his curly yellow hair. He was often out in the streets of Nidaros. Eilífr had seen him first three days after their arrival, limping up the the cathedral aisle to say his prayers at the high altar. In ignorance, he stepped forward to offer his arm to this small, hunched boy who seemed barely able to walk unaided. Instantly, two guards had stepped forward to lay heavy hands on his arms. The boy had looked up at him, and given a sweet smile. 'My thanks, stranger, but I must walk this path by my own strength, and with St Olav's aid.'

Eilífr had bowed, and stepped back, but the boy had joined him in his pew on his way out of the cathedral, asking where he had come from, and listening with interest to all he could tell him of Shetland.

'That's typical of him,' Saebjörn said. 'He's good with the common people.'

'I took him for a boy until he spoke.'

'He's fifteen. He wasn't born with his hunched back and withered foot. One story says that he was carried into battle when he was a baby, the old civil wars, and held in that shape too long, and another blames a maid who dropped him.' Saebjörn glanced over his shoulder again. 'Inge Krokrygg, his enemies call him, but he's good with the people, and he listens to the counsellors.'

'Perhaps he has to,' Eilífr said, 'since his mother leads them.' His own father had died when he was a youngster, and there were times he thought his mother still saw him as a ten-year-old. Although all the work of the farm was in his charge, she would give orders before he had had the chance to decide what he wanted to do. Perhaps she would take a step back once he had a wife ... he smiled as he thought of Lína's sky-blue eyes and sweet mouth. He would ask for her when he reached home again — and surely the earl would return after this feast, unless he was persuaded to stay by the start of the hunting season. Eilífr checked a sigh. He had come to like his genial, poetic lord, but there was no denying Rögnvaldr was easily swayed by a whim. It would take only one of these kings to say, 'Come, Rögnvaldr, help us chase the bears out of the woods!' and they'd be here until the river froze over, and their ship was trapped by the ice until the spring thaw.

It was the third king who was likely to do that, King Sigurd Munn. He had much in common with the earl himself, the restlessness, and the ungovernable nature — except that the earl could be reasoned with, and gossip said that King Sigurd could not. He was stout and strong, with light brown hair, and an ugly mouth in an otherwise well-shaped face. Every movement was brisk: his walk, his gestures, the

54

way he mounted his horse and rode off. He was an expert with the sword, the axe, the bow, and had been talking for some weeks of the sport they'd have in the hunting season.

On the thought, King Sigurd's voice roared out, exactly as he'd imagined. 'Well, Rögnvaldr, what say you to clearing these woods of bears?'

The earl laughed and rose. 'Not this year, my leige lord. I have graver business to prepare for.' He turned and bowed to the priest at the end of the table. 'While my lord Breakspear here has talked of Norway's own archbishop with you, he has inspired me with a greater dream.' He raised his glass, and looked around the hall. 'My men, what do you say to a crusade to the Holy Land?'

There was an astonished hush, then a buzz of voices. Saebjörn leapt to his feet, face alight with enthusiasm, blue-green eyes blazing. 'I say aye, my lord!' He led the cheer, and King Eystein rose to lift his glass in a toast to the enterprise.

The Holy Land! Eilífr felt a glow of excitement burn within him, warring with his desire to return home. In the market of this city he'd smelled strange spices, seen people with skin dark as autumn leaves under white turbans, and wondered what strange lands they came from. Now he would have the chance to see for himself. He leapt to his feet, and Saebjörn clapped him on the back. 'To our success!'

The men around them laughed and raised their glass funnels. Eilífr was beginning to know the faces; there were representatives of each king in this corner. Two were King Eystein's men, a hard-drinking Viking with unruly fair hair and the hammer of Thór on a thong around his neck, and his crony with a long scar slashed down one cheek. A group of three belonged to King Sigurd, brothers with dark hair and beards, who talked loudly of boar hunts and stag chasing in the forests of Scotland. Then there were two younger men that he took to be of King Inge's party, for they looked down their noses at the rowdy talk of hunting, and the right hand of one moved to his dagger when the Viking used the name Krokrygg.

A great gust of wind hammered at the roof, blotting out their talk. The Viking looked up at the ceiling, and laughed scornfully. 'Your

55

lily-livered Christ who let his enemies kill him has no power over Odin, it seems. Now the Wild Hunt is riding over our heads, with the appearances of the men who are to die this year.' He drained his glass. 'To Odin and the old gods! Shall we go and look for our own faces, as they pass over?' He turned to Eilífr. 'What say you, Shetlander? Will you come and look with us? Or will we lie on a grave together, and become seers?'

His scarred companion jerked his head up. 'Shetlander?'

'One of the earl's men, did you not know it?'

'I took no notice,' his companion retorted, and gave Eilífr a measuring look. His eyes narrowed. 'When did you come from there?'

'He came with the earl,' the Viking repeated. 'Where have your wits gone? They left at midsummer, after the Ting.'

'Did they, indeed?' The man ran his finger down the puckered scar, then raised his iron-grey eyes back to Eilífr. 'Perhaps you met a friend of ours there before you left.'

'He's a Christ-follower,' the Viking said. 'He'll know nothing.'

'He may have seen him.' The scarred man put a hand on the Viking's shoulder, to silence him, and leaned forward to Eilífr. 'Aldúlfr Arisson's his name. A tall man, friend, harsh-faced, with a long nose and slanted eyes under craggy brows. He was wearing an ochre cloak when I last saw him, lined with skin from reindeer he brought down with his own bow, and a blue tunic.'

'A reindeer's no shot for a man,' one of the dark men put in. 'A boar now, that'll test your courage, when it comes charging at you.'

The scarred man ignored him. 'Have you seen him, friend?'

Eilífr shook his head. 'I don't remember hearing of any strangers at the Ting, except for Earl Rögnvaldr's men. What was your friend doing in the isles? If you tell me who he might have been with, that could jog my memory.' His strongest memory of the Ting was of that heart-pounding run for his life, his leg stabbing with pain at every step, and the rough feel of the steeple-stone under his hand, the relief flooding through him to know that he'd made it, when he'd expected Lingormr to overtake him at the last moment. Yes, and the evening after the feast, with his arm around Lína's slim waist, kissing her in the summer twilight, and exchanging promises.

The scarred man jerked back from him, the Viking leaned forward. 'Do you enquire into our affairs, Shetlander?' His eyes glittered dangerously in the firelight.

Eilífr's heart thudded, but he held his head up proudly. 'I had affairs of my own at the Ting. I ask you to help my memory.'

'And you do not drink,' the scarred man said. The Viking began to rise, hand going to his dagger. At the other side of the table, King Inge's friends rose also.

Saebjörn clapped Eilífr's shoulder. 'Eilífr, friend.' Saebjörn stopped there, as his eyes met those of the Viking.

'Your friend is too sober,' the scarred man said smoothly. 'I think he does not like our king's ale.'

Saebjörn threw back his head and laughed. 'He is but lately come from Shetland. They brew only a weak and watery ale. I'll teach him to appreciate the king's. Eilífr, come and meet my friend Arni.' He thrust an arm into Eilífr's, and drew him into the shadows. 'We must move your place, friend, for you've made dangerous enemies. What were they asking you?'

'He described a man, and wanted to know if I'd seen him.'

'Tall and dark, with a rough face?' Eilífr nodded, and Sacbjörn looked grave. 'I know them of old. They herd together, and one of the three is missing, nobody seems to know where. But they are King Eystein's men, and wherever he's been lost, it would have been on the king's business.'

'Would the counsellors not investigate an official gone missing?'

'I didn't say he was an official. A spy, on business the king does not want known.'

'And business,' Eilífr said slowly, 'connected with Shetland. But why would King Eystein want to send a spy there?'

Chapter Six

Yule festivities

Lund, Unst.
Yolmanudur, Yule month, 1150.

They had given up hope of seeing Eilífr again this year as the nights darkened and the cold strengthened, when suddenly on one bonny, crisp day, when the hills were rust-pink with withered heather, the moors purple-red with spagnum moss, he and his brother Björn came striding over the hill and past the tall finger of Bordastubble Stone. Rannveig and her father were in the booth, carving. It was Faider who noticed him first: 'There're two young fellows coming this way, and I think one will get a king's welcome. You look, Ranka, your eyes are better than mine.'

It took her only a glance to recognise his walk. She hurried around the house to the annexe, where the girls were combing wool. 'Lína, come quickly!' She pointed. 'Look!'

Lína started incredulously, then gasped, and began to run forward. 'Eilífr!'

'And there's no need for you to be staring, Káta,' Rannveig said. 'Go and put some oatcakes on to cook, and pour a beaker of ale. The man will be thirsty after he's answered all our questions.'

Björn arrived at the house before the lovers, and greeted Rannveig awkwardly. His voice was breaking, she noticed, going suddenly from his child's high note to the man's voice it would become, and hearing it change he blushed, and fell silent. He was a good-looking boy, as dark as Eilífr, with strongly-marked eyebrows, and a stubborn chin.

'So,' she said, smiling, 'he's come home at last.'

Björn nodded. 'He saw Jakob of Norwick's knarr in Kirkwall, and offered to pull an oar homewards.'

There was a dark thong tucked into the neck of his tunic, like the one the dead man had worn. Björn caught her staring, and Rannveig decided to brazen it out. Let him think her as gossipy as his own mother, if he liked! 'I was wondering what was on your necklace.'

'This?' He drew it out, to show a silver cross, except that the cross hung on a paler strip of leather, and his hand covered the darker thong, fingers tucking it deeper into his tunic as he drew the cross out. 'My mother gave it to me last Yule.'

But what was on the other thong? She could not demand to see it, and rose, cheeks reddening at her own curiosity. It was none of her business. 'A kind gift. Will you take a beaker of ale, while we wait for Eilífr and Lína to remember about us?'

They came up to the house at last, Lína clutching Eilífr's arm, tears of happiness on her cheeks. Eilífr was taller and broader-shouldered than he had been, Rannveig thought, with a man's look in his face. 'Come in and sit down.'

'I'll sit on your briggistane, if I may.' He gave a long look out and around at the bright water, the rust-coloured hills. 'Ah, this is a view that's good to see.'

'But you must have seen so many exciting things,' Káta said. 'Tell us!'

He did his best: the voyage across the Norwegian sea in Earl Rögnvaldr's warship, their arrival in Nidaros, the feasting, the tall houses and the great stone cathedral, the magnificence of the court. 'But now I am home again, thanks to Jakob of Norwick.'

Lína hugged his arm to her. 'And Lingormr's family are keeping in seclusion, so you need not fear to stay here.'

He reddened at that, and changed the subject, feeling in his pouch for a small bundle, wrapped in cloth. 'This is for you, a pair of brooches from Nidaros. I got a pin for each of the girls, and a knife for Fasti.' He lifted his head and smiled. 'And nothing for you, Ranka, for someone else sent this gift, to check that you hadn't forgotten him in all these months.'

She felt the blood rush to her cheeks as she held out her hand for the parcel.

'Ranka's blushing!' Káta said. 'Of course she hadn't forgotten. Every so often she goes all dreamy, or stands in the doorway staring at the sailor's star, and we know she's thinking of him.'

'And why shouldn't she?' Manga said. 'He's very handsome. I'd marry him like a shot, if he asked me.'

'I'll wait until I'm asked,' Rannveig said tartly, but her hands trembled as she unwrapped the gift. It was a pair of brooches, made of brass that gleamed like gold, with a frilled edge and a lattice pattern on the back. She turned one over, admiring the craftsmanship. Not even Kristin of Lund had finer! She tried to keep her voice casual. 'Is Saebjörn living in Orkney over the winter?'

'He was hoping to come to Shetland with me, but the Earl has him fully occupied down in Orkney over the winter, re-fitting his boats.' Eilífr shot a quick glance at the look of disappointment she tried to conceal. 'But the Earl is to send him in the spring. Now, tell me all your news.' His arm tightened round Lína's waist. 'What feasts, what excitement?'

'The usual feasts at Winternights,' Lína replied. She smiled. 'It was no fun without you.'

'The dead man in the summer, just after you went,' Manga said. Rannveig felt Björn's arm go tense beside hers. 'Has your mother told you all about him?'

Eilífr shook his head.

'She was too busy exclaiming at how he'd grown, and lamenting over his clothes,' Björn said. 'And giving him a list of work to do now he was home again.'

Eilífr ignored him. 'A stranger?'

'A stranger, and one of importance,' Rannveig said. Eilífr's head went up; he nodded as she described him.

'I know who the man you mean is. I heard about him at the feast of Winternights, in Nidaros. Aldúlfr Arisson, they called him.' He described King Eystein's two followers, and their enquiries about their missing friend. 'They said he'd been here at the Ting.'

'But what interest,' Rannveig said, just as he had, 'would King Eystein have in what's going on in Unst?' She didn't look at Björn, but she could hear that he was holding his breath.

'They don't get on,' Eilífr said. 'Well, three kings reigning at once, what would you expect? He might be planning to take charge, and sent the man to go around the landowners and see who might be willing to support him.' He shook his head. 'But I don't see how support in Unst would be any good to him in Nidaros, unless he was hoping for men and ships.'

'And why,' Manga added, 'would that be so important that he was killed for it?'

ᚠᚠᚠᚠᚠ

The twelve days of feasting began in the middle of Yolmanudur, on the winter solstice. As a Christian community, they didn't do the things Amma remembered from her Norwegian girlhood, sacrificing a wild boar to Freya for a good growing season, or decorating trees with food and miniature clothes to entice the tree spirits back in spring, but on Solstice Eve, the children had left their shoes out, and a sheaf of hay beside them for Slepinir, and Rannveig had put presents in them: a carved boat for Fasti, with a red sail, and a cloth baby for Fjörleif, with a painted face and wool plaits. Both playthings had been a huge success. Fasti had run straight away to sail his boat across the ducks' pond by Amma's house, and Fjörleif had stared at her baby, one finger in her mouth, until Manga had reassured her that it really was meant for her. Manga had sewn the baby's blue dress while Káta had teased out the sheep's wool for its hair, and Lína had fashioned the boat's sail.

Rannveig had cherished those evenings, working together in the firelight, with Faider whittling the tiny oars, for they would be their last winter together. Lína and Eilífr were bound to marry this year, now Lína was sixteen, and their family circle would be broken – that is, everyone expected that they would marry, although lately she'd noticed a brittle touchiness about Lína, as if there had been some quarrel. Perhaps, Rannveig had reflected, pausing in her work to look at Lína's golden head bent over the red cloth, her sister was thinking twice about having to live with Márgret of Vinstrick. Perhaps she should have a word with Eilífr, and ask him how he intended to deal with his mother when he took a wife.

On Solstice Day, Faider insisted they roll the burning Sunwheel down the hill below their house, with Fasti and Fjörleif chasing after it, stumbling and shrieking with laughter, until it bounced clear from the bank over the beach and plunged hissing into the sea. 'A good omen,' Faider had said, ruffling Fasti's hair. 'Now we can be sure the sun will come back. Do you think Rannveig remembered the sun cakes?'

'I helped,' Fjörleif said, taking his other hand. 'I made the thumb marks around the edges.'

They'd made the cakes with oats and honey, and after the sunwheel rolling Rannveig baked them on the flat stone by the fire, and they shared them, squealing at burnt fingers. That evening, as it grew dark, they walked the boundary of the croft, with Faider and Rannveig each carrying a burning branch, Faider at the head of the procession, Rannveig leading up the rear, and the other girls carrying oil lamps inside an animal skull. Fasti and Fjörleif capered around them, banging drums made of stretched sheepskin. Around them, all their neighbours were doing the same, the rectangle of each croft being outlined in fire, the rattle of drums echoing across the bay.

'There!' Fasti said with satisfaction, as they came back into the house. 'Now the trolls will know to keep clear of us.'

After that, they burned the Yule log, a great branch Faider had hauled up from the beach, decorated with sprigs of greenery, and carved with runes. The last piece of it had been wrapped in cloth and put up in the rafters, ready to light next year's fire.

The solemn feast of Christmas was three days later, with Midnight Mass in the church, where they welcomed the Christ-Child into the world with flickering oil lamps and rush dips, and then the second mass at mid-day, followed by a feast at the house of Nikolas of Lund. Faider led the way up the hill with Amma on his arm, then Káta and Manga, giggling and whispering to each other. Rannveig and Lína had little Fjörleif between them, her eyes round with excitement. Manga had brushed her gold hair until it shone, and wound long strips of blue cloth into her plaits, and she wore her sea-green bead between two new brooches that Faider had bought from a passing tinker. Fasti capered around them, waving his wooden sword. 'If Odin and his Wild Hunt should come,' he boasted, 'I'll chase them away.'

Amma crossed herself and looked fearfully up at the sky. 'Don't joke about such things, boy. The old gods haven't gone so far away.'

'It's just Amma's old superstitions,' Rannveig whispered to Fjörleif. 'Don't be scared.'

'Not so superstitious that I've taken to imagining things,' Amma said in her ear. 'I saw lights at the Bordastubble Stone, last Winternights.'

Rannveig stopped walking to stare at her. Amma nodded significantly. 'Some people keep the old ways.'

There was no time to ask more, for Nikolas was on the briggistanes to greet them. 'Reifr, come in, come in! Amma, I hope you've not tired yourself coming all this way. Go right to the fire. Rannveig, lass, bonnier than ever, and with a fine suitor, I'm hearing. Lína!' He kissed her soundly on the cheek, and laughed at her blush. 'That's for Eilífr, until he arrives to give you it for himself. And do I hear a story of two brothers courting two sisters, Káta? Come in, come in, all of you, and eat your fill.'

They seated themselves on benches. The two long boards were curved with the weight of food on them: a pig, still whole, with an apple in its mouth, cauldrons of boiled beef, shanks of mutton in a sauce flavoured with thyme from the hillside. Father Jóhann said grace, and the feast began, interrupted by toasts, for Nikolas of Lund enjoyed raising his glass to every person or enterprise that crossed his mind. It was soon time, Rannveig thought, to take the children out. Fasti was reaching that over-excited stage that meant he wouldn't sleep at all, and Fjörleif was flushed and starting to be tearful at each roar of appreciation.

Although their home was only ten minutes walk away, they were staying the night, for there was no moon, and Nikolas preferred to fill his house with people all evening, rather than see it empty at first dusk. An annexe had been set aside for the women, and filled with hay beds. Rannveig chose a haybed near the door, and coaxed the children into it. Fjörleif settled without a murmur, right thumb going straight into her mouth, left hand clutching her precious green bead, but Fasti insisted on a story. Rannveig told him Noah's ark, allowing him to name all the animals until his voice drained away to a sleepy murmur, then laid her cloak gently over them.

'They're sweet,' a voice murmured. It was Geira, the youngest daughter of Nikolas of Lund, in her middle twenties now, with dark hair, lips red as raspberries, and an intense, sulky face. She had reason for it, Rannveig knew – the whole of Unst knew. She was the plainest of Nikolas's daughters, and instead of giving her a larger dowry, her parents had decided to keep her at home to take care of them in their old age. Rannveig visited her from time to time, with lively Fasti and Fjörleif at her heels. She'd seen how wistfully the other girl watched the children playing, and pitied her.

Rannveig smiled at her. 'Sweet wasn't the word I used when the pair of them came chasing through my baking yesterday.'

'But you wouldn't be without them,' Geira said. She slanted a malicious look at Rannveig's moss-green apron-skirt and gleaming brooches. 'Though rumour says you're hoping for a house of your own – in Orkney, maybe, in the Earl Rögnvaldr's household?'

Her hopes were too precious to discuss. 'They're a handful. I couldn't leave them until Manga and Káta are old enough to run the household. ' She smiled at Geira. 'You see, Faider needs me as much as your parents need you.'

'They don't need me,' Geira said, jutting her lip petulantly. 'Look at my father, alert, busy, keeping his finger on the gossip here. What need has he of a daughter? Or my mother, in charge of the house, and if she wasn't taking the reins then Maria would be only to glad to step in and start ordering everyone about – she does enough of that already. I do nothing that a maid couldn't do, and while I wait here, my life is running away from me.'

On the hay, Fjörleif sighed, and moved her hand. Geira smiled, and bent over her, then jerked back. Her eyes stared in the flickering light of the kolli lamp; the colour drained from her face, leaving her rosy lips bloodless. Her hand came up to her breast. Rannveig put a hand on her shoulder, alarmed. 'What's wrong?'

Geira clutched at the line of beads strung between her shoulder brooches. Her hand was white against the brightness of scarlet and cobalt flowers, combed white glass, spun sea green with silver flecks, gold-sparked brown. She shrugged Rannveig's hand away, and turned from her. 'It's hot in here.' Her voice was higher than usual. 'Let's get some air. They're sleeping now.'

Spun sea-green glass... Rannveig looked down at the children. The light flickered on Fjörleif's gold plaits, her chubby neck, the spun sea-green bead on its thong – the bead she had found in the broch, where the dead man had lain.

ᚠᚠᚠᚠᚠ

After the Christmas feasting, it was the time of the guizers, and Fasti was full of importance, for his best friend Petr, his companion at Father Jóhann's lessons each morning, had asked him to join the skekklers, and Faider had agreed that he could go, so long as he behaved.

'Stand still!' Rannveig told him, as she tied him into the straw costume: straw around each leg, fastened at ankle, knee and thigh with horsehair twine, a great sheaf of it over his tunic, more down his arms, fastened at shoulder, elbow, wrist. 'You'll wear yourself out before you've even started.' She was doubtful about how well he'd manage, even if he was only doing the first half of the round, Lund House, Bordastubble, and back to Underhoull. She hoped Faider would still remember he had a tired little boy with him, once the ale started flowing. She wished she could go herself to look after him, but only men were allowed to be skekklers. Fjörleif, excluded from the fun, nursed her doll in the corner.

'There,' Manga said, holding up his conical hat. 'Put that on, and see if you can see.'

His voice came from inside the straw that covered his face. 'Not very well.'

Fjörleif forgot her sulks and came to laugh at him. 'You look like a walking col of hay.' She parted the straw to peer at him. 'Can you see

68

now?'

'Just. Can you fetch me my sword?'

She ran to get it for him. While Rannveig had been dressing Fasti, Lína and Káta had been tying straw around Faider. 'Finished!' Lína said. 'Do you have his hat, Manga?'

'Stand together, so we can look at you!' Rannveig ordered.

Faider and Fasti shuffled together, Faider's head bent forward to avoid knocking his hat off on the roof. 'Now you've plenty of ale for when we arrive here?'

'Plenty,' Rannveig assured him, between giggles. They looked so strange, these walking straw men with their high, conical hats. 'Be off with you.'

Odin's wagon was well tilted in the sky when they returned. Rannveig heard the music floating on the wind, the wooden whistle and the banging drum, and looked out to see the torches winding their way across the path from Bordastubble. The table was piled high with oatcakes, bread, meat, and cheese. Her sisters were ready at their posts, and Fjörleif had been given a small jug of ale to pour for Fasti. It would not be such a feast as Nikolas of Lund had given, but they need not be ashamed of their hospitality either.

Soon there was laughter from outside. Rannveig flung the door open, and they capered in, nine men dressed in their straw clothing, with the conical hats covering their faces. Among them, Rannveig knew only Fasti, by his height, the smallest of them. They danced around the room to the sound of the whistle, and Faider told some riddles, and another man recited part of a poem about the deeds of St Olav. Then they sat down, and while they ate, Olav of Bordastubble told a long story about the wars of the first King Olav, and how Norway had become Christian.

The girls were kept busy, serving ale and pressing meat and bread on the guests. The Skekklers kept their masks on, brushing the hanging staw aside to eat, eyes glittering through the stalks. Rannveig was walking around the end of the boards when she almost stumbled over a man's outstretched legs. She clutched at the board, recovering herself, while he drew his legs back with a gesture of apology.

For a moment her breath stopped. It was the boot, at last. She was sure of it. His legs had been stretched out towards the fire, with the right foot crossed over the left ankle, and the sole of the boot tilted upwards. He was here.

For the moment, she poured him more ale, and moved away, smiling. She would be able to tell more about him when he rose. Not Olav of Bordastubble, not Faider, not Eilífr, who was at the other end of the table, with Lína hovering attentively. She kept watching, and at last her man stretched his feet to the fire once more. She came around in front of him, platter on hip. Yes, it was the sole she'd copied. When they thanked her and rose, she tried to keep him under her eye, among all the others so similarly dressed. He wasn't as tall as Faider, and moved like a younger man, but she couldn't tell, under the thick straw, if he was bearded, or what colour his hair was.

She asked Faider casually the next day who the guizers had been, but it did not help her. All three of the men who'd hesitated to lay hand on the corpse had been there: younger Nikolas of Lund, Hafthór of Vigga and Björn, Eilífr's brother.

ᚠᚠᚠᚠᚠ

Chapter Seven

A Lovers' Quarrel

Now it was Thorri's month. 'The men's month,' Faider had teased, as Rannveig had gone outside on Hoggunótt, Midwinter Night, feeling foolish, to drop a curtsey, hold the door open wide, and invite the frost giant in. 'Pagan superstitions,' she remembered Mother saying, and Faider had laughed, as he was doing now, and said, 'I'll expect all you girls to run around me for the whole month. My rivlins warmed at the fire, and a beer pot always in my hand.'

'You can expect,' Rannveig said, closing the door against the cold.

'If I get,' Faider said, 'then you can expect too, in Gói's month.'

Thorri had come indeed. The frost sparkled on the hill, and separated the grass stems on the top of the felly dyke around the house. In the bay of Lund below her, the frilled seaweed glittered at the sea's edge, and the water was a cold, hard blue. Rannveig pulled her shawl around her shoulders and stood up, flexing her fingers. It was too cold to sit outside, carving the clibber bowls and pots that they sold, but she could hardly see inside, with the doors curtained by sheepskins to keep out the winter cold, and she wanted to take special care with these bowls: a set of six, commissioned by Jakob of Norwick for his summer blót. After she had finished them, she intended to carve a set for herself. He would try to visit in spring, Saebjörn had told Eilífr. They could not be wed so quickly, of course, for she could not leave the children to Manga and Káta just yet, but another year, two, and she could marry, to look after her husband, rather than her father, and have children of her own clinging to her skirts.

Fasti came out now, his red-sailed longship clutched in his arms. 'Ranka, I'm just going to sail my boat.'

'Don't wade in deep now,' Rannveig said. 'It's too cold. No deeper than your knees. Promise?'

Fasti sighed. 'Promise. And my boat won't sink, like the other one.'

'It won't sink, if you set it on the water carefully.' Rannveig frowned, and a snatch of children's play came into her mind. When she'd found Fasti and Fjörleif playing at killing the dead man in the broch, she'd been distracted by the green bead which told her the dead man had met a woman there. Now, she recalled, Fasti had said something about a boat. She searched her memory as she watched him stomp down the hall towards Amma's house. '*Now I strike you with my dagger,*' he'd crowed at Fjörleif, '*and you fall dead, and I run away in my boat.*'

She rose, and hurried down the hill after him. 'Fasti, what boat are you talking about, that sank?'

'The man took it out to sea, then there was hammering, then it started to sink, and sink, and the water went over the sides, and there was a sound like this – ' he gulped loudly 'and the sea ate it, mast and all.'

Rannveig caught at his arm as he tried to run away. 'No, wait, Fasti. What man? When?'

Fasti shrugged. 'I couldn't really see who it was. He took the boat out, and rowed it round into Lunda Wick, so he was too far to see.'

'Took the boat from the geo?'

'It was in the geo.' He flushed, and hung his head. 'I saw it, and I thought maybe if nobody took it away I could take it out round the bay, when you weren't looking. It was a good boat.'

'You know you're not allowed to take the boat out by yourself,' Rannveig said automatically. The stranger's boat! 'Was it a big boat, like Nikolas of Lund's?'

Fasti shook his head. 'Not as big as a knarr, but bigger than our faerling. It had a mast and a sail, but they were laid flat, that's why I didn't see it until I went over the headland to see if it was still there.' He waved past the broch.

'When did you see this boat?'

'The day after the man died.' Fasti tugged his arm away from her grasp. 'And the next day, then I got up early.' He flushed again. 'Well, you wouldn't have let me take it out if you'd been up. But the man was already taking it. He poled it out of the gap between the rocks, and rowed round the headland, then the sea ate it, and he swam ashore. Can I go to Amma's pond now?'

'Don't get too wet.' Rannveig watched as he scampered down the hill, her mind weighing up the implications of what he'd seen. So the man they'd found dead had come in a boat, and pulled it up into the beach, mast down, so that it would be hidden, and then somone else, his killer, had taken the boat and scuttled it, another barrier to recognising him. A smaller boat than Nikolas of Lund's; that suggested stealthy business round the isles, before the stranger was picked up by a sea-going boat to return to the court. She wondered if Eilífr's suspicions were right, if King Eystein was planning to depose the other kings, and rule alone. If he was approaching the important landowners to see what support he'd have, then he must have been meeting Thórfastr of Vigga or Nikolas of Lund.

Rannveig looked across at Lund. Somehow she didn't see genial, hospitable Nikolas of Lund being involved in intrigue. He was too proud of his standing in the community, with links of kinship to all the principal families of the place. Yet those very links might make him a good man to win over, in the hope that he'd bring others with him.

His son Nikolas was more likely. Chafing at being under his father's governance still, his wife resentful of her secondary place in the house, he might be open to suggestions of rebellion, with the bribe of a king who'd reward him for his support. Yet, if that was the case, why would he kill the king's messenger?

ᚠᚠᚠᚠᚠ

It was two days later that Rannveig looked up from her carving, and saw Geira of Lund walking over the Ness of Vinstrick towards Underhoull, a woven-rush basket on one arm, and her amber cloak clutched round her against the chill wind. She wore stout leather boots, and her dark hair was covered with a knitted kerchief. Rannveig set her bowl aside and cleaned her tools, then went to the yaird dyke to meet her.

'We were baking,' Geira said, 'and made far too much.' She held

75

the basket out: three round loaves, wrapped in cloth. 'I thought these might save you a baking day.'

Rannveig accepted them with thanks, and showed her into the dimness of their main room, lit only by the glow from the peat fire. 'Come and sit down, and tell me all the news with you.'

Geira laid her cloak aside, and flicked her dark plaits back over her shoulders. The shadows brought out her strong cheekbones, the low, dark brows, the sulky, determined jut of her lips. Today she wore an ochre underdress, and a blood-red apron-skirt over it, with cream finger-braid round the neck and hem. The necklace she had worn on the last feast of Winternights hung between her shoulder brooches. The beads gleamed in the firelight: white, amber, green. Geira saw Rannveig looking at them, and gave a long sigh. 'You knew, didn't you? I saw you noticing, when I realised that little Fjörleif had found my bead. You were always a quick one.' She put up her hand to clasp the beads. 'I thought I'd gathered them up, and, well, if I had missed one or two, it wouldn't matter. There was nothing to connect me with the broch. Anyone could have lost them.'

'She and Fasti were playing,' Rannveig said, 'and Fjörleif fell, and found it.'

Geira leaned forward. Her dark eyes were bright in the dim light. 'I don't mind you knowing – I know you won't tell my father, and oh, it will be a relief to tell someone at last. I've been so unhappy!' The tears glistened, spilled over onto her lower lashes, and one ran down her cheek, but her voice remained steady. 'And I know you'll believe I didn't kill him.'

'Tell me what happened,' Rannveig said. 'How did you come to meet Aldúlfr Arisson?'

Geira took a deep breath. 'It was in Scotland. My father had business there, oh, years ago, when I was only a girl, not old enough yet to think of marriage, before King Eystein had gone to Norway. His mother, Bjaðök, was some kind of cousin of my mother's, through her father – that's how we came to meet the king and his friends. Aldúlfr was one of them, and he – ' Her cheeks reddened. 'Oh, he teased me, the way an older man does, and I was flattered he made a pet of me so.' Her red lips turned down; her voice became harsh. 'I think that even then he had his eye on a dowry. He was a landless man, and if he could win me over, my father might consider him a match for me. He was bold, and strong-featured, and when they staged fights for amusement he was often a winner.'

She paused, eyes sparkling as she remembered. 'We were there when the Norwegian lords came to tell Eystein that his father had died, and had named him as his son. He went off with them, of course, but Aldúlfr told me that he wouldn't forget me, that I'd see him in Shetland. We had a sign – already, we had a sign, a white pebble left by the door, that meant I was to meet him after dark in the bay.' She bit her lip. 'I thought that was so romantic.' She flushed. 'Well, I was too young for a lover, so I couldn't expect that he would talk to my father for me yet, and it was exciting! He didn't come for two years, until I was fifteen, and then one day I saw the pebble lying by the door, and knew it was his signal. I waited until all the household was in bed, then I crept out, down to the bay, under the shadow of the church, and it *was* him! I couldn't believe it at first, that it was really him, come back to me. I wanted him to stay, and meet my parents, and be a proper suitor.' She curled her lip. 'Oh, already I'd heard people saying what a pity it was that I wasn't as pretty as my sister! And here he was, older, and distinguished, and dressed like a man of the court...' A sob caught in her throat. 'Dressed as he was when you found his body.'

She broke down in tears, and Rannveig put an arm round her shoulders, heart wrung with pity. Poor Geira, to have carried this burden of grief and guilt alone these seven months! But the older girl rubbed her eyes and sat back.

'He had all sorts of excuses why he couldn't speak to Faider yet. He said he didn't doubt I'd wait for him, that the king had promised him an estate that would let him keep a wife, but he was too valuable to him to let go yet. But he was so loving... we kept meeting, every two or three months in the summer. He kept a small boat in Skaillvarg, and he would come over on a trading ship, and then sail up here. Usually he was alone, though sometimes he had two

77

companions, a tall fair Viking and a shorter man with a scar down one cheek.'

Rannveig's heart jolted. The exact description of the men who had given Eilífr the dead man's name! But what, in St Olav's name, were these three doing here?

'Did they,' she asked hesitantly, 'come just to see you? Or did they visit others while they were here?'

'I thought it was just to see me,' Geira said. 'Oh, no doubt they had business in Skaillvarg too, or trading round the isles, but he told me that he came only to see me. Oh, Rannveig, if I could make you understand! It was me, *me* – he was the only person who was interested. He'd ask all about what I'd done in the last months, since I'd seen him, and all the gossip of the isles, what had happened at the small Ting here, and the big Ting at Tingwall – because it concerned me, nothing was too boring for him to want to know.'

Spying for the king, Eilífr had said. Rannveig's heart felt cold. Geira might believe he'd come all this way for her, but the harsh features she'd carved hadn't been those of a man who'd do that just for love. 'Did he come alone, that last time?'

Geira began to cry in earnest. 'Oh, Rannveig, our last meeting! I got his signal, the day we came back from the Ting, and came to meet him at the broch. It wasn't quite dark, but I hoped that everyone would be tired enough not to waken as I went out. He was waiting for me.' Rannveig said nothing; Geira's hand turned under hers, and clung. 'I told him all that had happened at the Ting, about how Patrekr of Baliasta had been murdered, and Eilífr arrested, and how the Earl had released him, and Lingormr of Vigga had been hanged instead.' Her voice faltered. 'Then I told him a lie. It was all my fault! I wish now that I had never done it, but you see, I was so tired of waiting.' She laid her free hand on her belly. 'I said that I was with child, and that I wanted to go with him, now, rather than face the shame of it. I begged him to take me away with him, but he refused. It was a horrid argument, we were hissing at each other, because we didn't dare speak louder, in case you heard us here at Underhoull, and we didn't want to set your dog barking – he knew me, of course, and he obeyed when I told him to lie down and be quiet, but he was suspicious of Aldúlfr.' She turned her head away, and sighed. 'He didn't believe me about the child, or he didn't believe it was his, and he said he wasn't taking me anywhere, and I could bear the shame of my own behaviour, and he wished he'd never seen me, and then he caught hold of me, and I hit him, and wrenched myself away, and that's when my necklace broke. I caught at the ends, and felt on the ground for the beads, and all the time he was saying horrible, horrible things, and I just couldn't bear it. I picked up my skirts and ran away from him.' Her face became bleak. 'Then the next thing I knew was that you came to say you had found him dead. Well, I didn't know what to do! How could I bear to have him buried, nameless like that – yet how could I own up to knowing him? I hoped Faider would recognise him, from Scotland, and name him, but he didn't ... that is, I think he didn't, but perhaps he suspected me, and wanted to keep my name out of it, and so he just pretended not to know him. He hasn't said anything to me, not asked any questions. And since Faider didn't recognise him, I just had to pretend he was as much a stranger to me as he was to everyone else.'

'Listen,' Rannveig urged. 'Was he alone, this time, or were his friends with him?'

Geira shook her head. 'I didn't see anyone else – I don't think they were with him.' She bit her lower lip again. 'But I did think someone was there – when we were arguing – I thought I heard stones move – I said so to Aldúlfr, and we both listened, but there was nothing.' Her eyes slid sideways to meet Rannveig's. She rose suddenly, shaking her skirts smooth. 'I must go. I'll be missed. They'll wonder why I was away so long.' She bundled her cloak about her, and turned for a last confidence. 'Now, though, I think that someone was there – the person who killed him.' Her eyes sparked, her dark head went up. 'And I'll avenge him. There is only me to do it. Nobody notices me watching and listening, but some day, someone will drop a word amiss, and then I'll know. I'll *know*.'

'Perhaps,' Rannveig thought, watching her out of sight. Yet it could have been a different story. Geira had described a bitter quarrel, in which she'd begged Aldúlfr to take her away. If he'd really cared about her, he'd have done it. For all her seeming naivety, Geira wasn't stupid. Face to face with the way her lover had strung her along all these years, she could have been angry and disillusioned enough to have taken the dagger from his belt and struck him with it.

It seemed likely ...but if that was the way it had been, then who was the mysterious man Fasti had seen scuttling the boat – the man who'd left the footprint she'd traced?

Chapter Eight

The Fleet sets Sail

The light had returned at last, thin at first, in a series of cloudy days, then one morning Rannveig woke to see watery sunshine creeping around the edges of the door. The blackbird was singing on the roof, a series of chuckles. Rannveig rose, pulled her cloak around her, and went out to breathe the fresh morning air. The sea was glass-calm below her, and in spite of the sun, it was cold enough yet for there to be a glazing of ice where the Burragarth burn ran down to the sea.

Rannveig looked across at the little cluster of houses, with the bigger hall of Nikolas of Lund in the centre. She was still reflecting on what Geira had told her of her relationship with the dead man. Geira had seen it as a love affair, but Rannveig didn't believe it. That a harsh-featured man like Aldúlfr Arisson, known in the Norwegian court as King Eystein's spy, should spend several years courting a daughter of a minor landowner - no. She shook her head. Oh, Nikolas of Lund was important here in Unst, but in the context of Norway, he was nobody! Arisson had had some other motive, and from Geira's talk it was obvious what it was: he was spying on what went on in Shetland. He'd asked her all about what happened at the Ting, about her family affairs, about all the local gossip: who was kin with whom, who friends, who at odds. Then, she supposed, he went back to Norway with his two friends, the tall Viking and the man with the scar, and reported it all to the king. She remembered Eilífr's description of King Eystein: dark, with a dingy complexion, and a covetous, narrow mouth, not one to give anything away without expecting a return. But what return could he expect from their small communities in Unst?

Another thought had struck her too. Geira had mentioned the dog, yet not asked what he was doing tied up in the old chapel. Surely that would have been a natural thing to ask, even in the recounting of that painful scene? Rannveig frowned, thinking it through. Geira wanted to run away with Arisson, and like every proud Norsewoman, she wouldn't want to come empty-handed. Suppose she'd found out, somehow, where their silver was buried? Had she been desperate

83

enough to steal from them? Yes, Rannveig thought, she'd been besotted enough to lay everything aside. But some remnant of fellow-feeling had made her take, not all, but half of their store. Or maybe that was all she could carry, or safely hide, and she'd meant to take more that night, but Oskur's presence had prevented her. Then after Arisson's death she'd returned it. She no longer needed her dowry, and she wouldn't have been able to explain the silver if it had been found in her room. Yes, it could have happened like that.

By the time she and Lína were fetching buckets of water from the burn, there was warmth in the sun. Rannveig stood for a moment, stretching her back, and enjoying this promise that summer was on its way. The equinox was but a couple of weeks away now, the spring equalling of light and darkness, and only three weeks after that would be Gaukmanudur, the cuckoo month - not that she had ever heard a cuckoo, but Amma had imitated it for her. Spring ... soon it would be time for travelling again, and perhaps Saebjörn would come.

'We must start preparations for your bridal,' she said to Lína. 'Do you want to be married in Eggtid, or wait for Solmanudur, and be sure of sunshine?'

Lína's fair skin flushed crimson. 'I'm not going to be married this summer.' Tears filled her blue eyes. 'Eilífr is going on a crusade, if you please, with that Earl Rögnvaldr that he thinks so much of.'

'A crusade!' Rannveig stared at her. 'To the Holy Land?'

'I've argued and argued with him. He won't listen.' Lína stamped her foot on the soft earth. 'He wants to go! He doesn't care that he's leaving me behind, or that we were to be married this year. He's all excited about seeing strange places, and going a-viking across the seas, and coming back rich. As if I cared for that! Oh, Rannveig, I'm afraid that he won't come back at all.' She set to crying in good earnest. Rannveig put an arm around her, sat her down on a rock, and petted and soothed until the sobs had died away.

'Lína, how long have you known all this?'

Lína shook her head. 'For ages - since Yule. He thought I'd be pleased! The shipbuilders are making a special ship for the Earl in Norway right now, with thirty oars and gold decoration, and they plan to sail early in the spring, along with ships from Orkney and Norway.'

Rannveig looked about her at the first blue-green grass hazing the dried gold clumps of last year's stems. 'So Eilífr will need to go down to Orkney soon, to join the Earl. Oh, Lína, why did you not tell me?'

'I hoped he would change his mind, but the more I argued with him, the more stubborn he became.' The corners of her mouth turned down. 'It's a woman's task to stay at home and wait. There's no use trying to stop them.'

'No,' Rannveig agreed, 'no use.' She wondered if Saebjörn would be going too, and knew that of course he would. As well try to bridle the sea as stop a man like that from going a-viking when the opportunity offered.

'And now,' Lína said, 'Jakob of Norwick is talking of a trading voyage to Orkney, to offer them beach-dried fish for their ships, and Eilífr says he will go with him, to join the Earl's ship, in case Saebjörn doesn't make it up, to fetch him and anyone else who wants to join the Earl.' Her face crumpled up again. 'Oh, Ranka, he says it will be at the next weather chance, in the next three weeks or so!'

This was a shock indeed. Rannveig crushed down her own disappointment, and sat back on the rock, considering. Yet perhaps it was as well that Eilífr and Lína hadn't married before he left; she couldn't see her gentle Lína coping with being a grass-widow in charge of a household, particularly Margret of Vinstrick's household, perhaps with a child at foot, or worse, being left a widow. This way, if Eilífr didn't come home - though St Olav grant that he may! - then she would be free to grieve, then look around her and love again.

Now was not the time to speak such practicalities. She set herself to soothe Lína and interest her in the tasks of the household: buckets to fill, bread to bake. 'And you know,' she coaxed, 'he has had a charmed life so far. Besides, you hear such tales of the East. Maybe he will come home with a chest of silver, and necklaces as gold as your hair to deck you in. Think of the pretty bride you'll be then!'

Einmanudur, one month until summer, 1151.

It was two weeks later when she saw a strange sail on the southerly horizon, not a knarr, but a light-weight galley, with eight oars and a red-brown sail. It came around the point of Lund and into the bay; the sail dropped, the oars backed, and the snake-prowed boat slid up the beach. Rannveig felt her heart thumping. It might not be him, of course... She watched eagerly as the men jumped out of the galley, assembled into lines and marched up to Lund. The leader had fair hair, and a proud, upright walk.

He would go to Nikolas of Lund first, to tell the Earl's errand and ask for volunteers for his crusade, then he would come to Underhoull. She set aside her carving, and ran into the annexe to find her comb, the brooches he had given her, and the green cloth that had been the Earl's gift. When he arrived he would find her ready.

By the time she saw him coming out of the house of Lund, the sun had crossed the sound, and was shining on the Yell hills, picking out the first green grass among the heather, the lime-green moss where the glinting burns had overflowed with the winter rain. The black and white shaldurs had returned, and were peep-peeping among the grass by the shore, stabbing it with their long beaks. As Lína had gone to meet Eilífr, so Rannveig went out to meet Saebjörn, her hair brushed and rippling down her back, the cloth of her moss-green apron-skirt gleaming softly in the sun. She did not run, as Lína had, for they were not yet on those terms, but walked sedately forward, watching him approach over the hill, and waited there at the corner of the out-field, breathing quickened, hands trembling.

He strode confidently over the hill, right up to her, and kissed her without hesitation, arms warm about her, then set her back from him to look at her. He was just as she'd remembered: the fair hair blowing about his face, the blue eyes that looked out at the horizon, the fair, level brows, the long, smiling mouth. She met his eyes shyly, and glanced down at the brooch on her shoulder. 'I'm wearing your gifts – thank you.'

They kissed again, then he put an arm around her waist and they walked together back to the house. 'Has Eilífr told you we're bound for the Holy Land? I was thinking to wed you and carry you off to Orkney, but it seems you'd be a lonely bride.'

'Eilífr and Lína have delayed their wedding. Lína's not best pleased, and his mother's rejoicing. That is, she's rejoicing at the delay, but not at his leaving.' Rannveig smiled. 'I think he'll be glad to get away. Between his mother's long face and Lína's, you'd think he was likely to drown the second he set foot in a boat.'

'And you?' He smiled back, teasing. 'I see no long face.'

'You don't look like a man who was born to be drowned. You'll be at the front of the battle, though. I hope my prayers will keep you safe there.'

'I knew you would make a good wife.' They were at the briggistane now, and Faider had come to welcome him, hastily scrambled into his best tunic, and the girls around him. He'd remembered their names, and had a smile for each.

'I hear you're assembling a fleet to go to the Holy Land,' Faider said. 'If I were but five years younger ... and without this brood to tend, of course.' He tousled Fasti's hair.

'I could go,' Fasti said. 'I was a skekkler this winter, Saebjörn, and it's boys' month, so I should be allowed to go.'

'You need to grow taller,' Saebjörn said. 'Two years, perhaps, then your legs would be able to reach the floor as you rowed.' He smiled. 'When we return.'

'Two years!' Lína said, dismayed. 'But Eilífr said you would be back in the autumn.'

'The Earl says that too, but I don't believe it. He's too curious.' Saebjörn's voice was resigned. 'We'll go to the southern lands, and then he'll want to go further, or he'll be delayed by writing poems to a beautiful woman, and then we'll have to winter there, and so it would be a pity to go no further when the summer comes again...' He smiled. 'I've served him since I was Fasti's age. His great-grandfather was also mine, so we are distant cousins.' He turned to Faider. 'Although my grandfather was a third son, and my father his second son, so that we have no land, and only the money we can make with our own hands. The Earl pays me well. After this voyage, if I come home safe – ' He crossed himself. ' – I'll have enough saved to buy a piece of land, when I settle, and more, if we're lucky in our venture.'

'I thought it was to be a crusade,' Rannveig said, 'not a raiding party.'

'Oh, I have no doubt we will combine the two.' Saebjörn frowned. 'All the same, I'm uneasy about leaving Orkney so unprotected. The Earl's reign there is secure enough, and I have every faith in his cousin, Harald Maddadarson – do you remember him, the young man who came to the Ting with him? - but too many of his strong men are coming on this venture with him.'

'I wonder ...' Rannveig said, and stopped. She thought for a moment, then began again. 'The dead man in the broch, did Nikolas of Lund tell you about him?' Saebjörn shook his head, and she told him the story. 'I could not think of a reason he would be here in Shetland, but if King Eystein was planning a raid on Orkney during Earl Rögnvaldr's absence, it would make sense to be sure of Shetland.'

'What of Svein Asleifsson?' Faider asked. 'Does the Earl trust him, after Earl Paul's death?'

'Oh, my lord is willing to trust anyone who will raise a glass with him. But yes, I think that for the moment there is peace between them.' He turned to Rannveig. 'As for your idea ... I will tell the Earl of it.'

ᚠᚠᚠᚠᚠ

Kirkwall, Orkney.
Einmanudur, one month until summer, 1151.

The fleet was assembled in the pool of water called the Peedie Sea, in the shadow of the great kirk that Earl Rögnvaldr had built in honour

88

of his murdered uncle, Magnus Erlendsson, Magnus the Martyr. All Orkney knew the stories of how the rocky site of his burial had become a green field, and everyone knew someone who had been healed there. Furthermore, Orkney's bishop, William the Old, had warned the people not to visit his grave, and been struck blind, until his sight had been miraculously restored by prayer at the very tomb he'd warned against. The Cathedral dominated the stone houses of the town, a high, cross-shaped building with a square tower that glowed fire-red in the early morning light. Below it, the ships were assembled, a fleet of fifteen longships, each flying a long pennant that rippled in the wind. Rögnvaldr 's own ship was the largest of them, with thirty-five rowing benches, and the prow and sides magnificently carved and gilded. Three of the other captains were Orcadians, and the rest were Norwegian lords.

'And a fine time we've had of it all winter,' Saebjörn told Eilífr, as they stood waiting for the Earl to come aboard. 'The Norsemen quarrelling with the local men, and the local men quarrelling back - did you hear, in Shetland, of the death of Arni Pin-Leg? He took malt and cattle from a farmer, then refused to pay him, so the farmer went to Svein Asleiflarson, who split Arni's head with an axe. The Earl had to pay compensation to Eindridi the Young, whose man he was. He's spent the winter paying compensation out of his own pocket, just to keep the peace. Thank goodness we're off at last.'

From the shore, the thin, trumpet note of the lur sounded four times, then a drum beat began. There was a stir among the local people watching, a passage made for the Earl, marching in ceremony down from his hall. The sun brightened his chestnut hair. He wore a leather jerkin over his amber velvet tunic, and waxed leather breeches and boots, ready for the voyage. A scarlet cloak swirled from his shoulders. He carried a wrought helmet under one arm, and a shield on the other. There was a younger man beside him, taller and strongly made, with a dark, ugly face. The Earl paused to embrace him before coming aboard.

'The Earl's young cousin,' Saebjörn said. 'Harald Maddadarson. He's shaping to be a fine chief, not handsome, but with a straightforward way about him, like the Earl himself, and they've all sworn allegience to him. There'll be peace in Orkney once we've got this lot away.' He crossed himself. 'I hope.'

The Earl raised his sword. The crowd cheered. The ropes were freed from the shore, and hauled aboard; the oars dipped and rose dripping, dipped again, and they were pulling away, through the neck of land and out into the bay. Soon the wind caught them; Rögnvaldr's men hauled the ropes until the ochre sail was tamed to a curve, and the foam hissed along the wooden sides. One by one, the other ships followed the golden ship north and east, around the headlands, then south into the sun.

Chapter Nine

Demand for a Blood-Price

It would soon be sadtid, seed time. The family had worked together to dell their rigs, and Rannveig and Lína had sifted through the saved seeds to find the best of them. 'Another week,' Rannveig said, laying her hand on the soil, 'and the earth will be ready.'

The light had flooded back into the world. Now the wide sky was blue, with rounded white clouds chasing each other in the summer breeze, and casting dappled shadows on the heather-dark hills. The first calves had been born in the byre, and the hill ewes were heavy with lamb. The burns ran chuckling to the sea between banks of yellow marsh marigolds, and the seabirds paired on the cliffs.

'And we'll need to watch Fasti,' Rannveig said, 'for he's determined to climb down after gull eggs, now he's heard the older boys boasting of it. Besides the danger, we have no need of them, now the hens are starting to lay.'

Suddenly, Lína gave a choked cry. 'It's Jakob of Norwick back, look! He'll have news.'

Rannveig turned. A ship was coming around Houllnan Ness, her sail bellied out in the light breeze, her prow pointing shorewards. Even as they watched, her red sail was gathered in and her yard lowered; ten pairs of oars dipped into the water. Rannveig leaned forward, shading her eyes against the sun. 'That's not Jakob of Norwick's knarr, his has only eight pair of oars.'

The ship was making for their own beach, the smaller half of the double curve that made Lunna Wick, rather than passing the headland of Vinstrick to come into the wide beach below the church. Rannveig felt an uneasiness in her stomach as she watched it make its way in so confidently. Grandmother's house was but fifty paces above the beach, and Fasti and Fjörleif were playing on the sand. 'Go and tell Faider that strangers are coming. I'll go down to Amma and the little ones.'

Lína turned to run around the house to the workshop. Rannveig scrambled downwards as quickly as she could, her heart thumping uncomfortably in her breast. They were good citizens of Norway, of course, with allegiance to the Kings, and had nothing to fear from strangers. All the same, she was glad to reach the beach and call the children to her before the blind prow touched the sand.

Amma had seen the ship and came out to her briggistane. Rannveig pulled Fasti and Fjörleif away, one hand in each of hers, and brought them up to stand by her.

'I want to see the knarr!' Fasti protested.

'Let us find out who it is, first, and what they want,' Rannveig said. 'For now, stay here beside me until Faider comes, then do as he says, immediately.' She and Amma stood shoulder to shoulder as the ship drew into the beach, Fasti's hand in Rannveig's, Fjörleif 's in Amma's. Amma said nothing, but her wrinkled hand was tight on the knobbed staff she used to help her walk. A man Rannveig took to be the ship's owner stood by the helmsman, looking around him, up at the broch, back to Amma's house, then up again, at their own house of Underhoull, across to the headland, and back to focus on her. The oars back-watered, the ship stopped, and the first men jumped overboard and hauled two ropes up the beach. The man aft shouted a command. Six more men splashed to the beach, then he himself followed.

He was very tall, with a shock of untidy fair hair. He wore a saffron tunic with an embroidered red band at the hem, brown trousers and a long cloak of dark grey. A knife dangled from his belt, hilt glinting in the sun. He paused for a moment on the beach, looking up at her still, then turned his head, waiting, as a second man, shorter, and muffled in a blue cloak, jumped over the ship's side and came to stand beside him. A moment's pause, then they came striding together, with the eight men formed in a square behind them. Rannveig felt her breath coming short. Her hands were trembling. She dared not look behind her to see if Faider was coming.

They came up at the burn mouth, taking long strides across the softened turf, then turned towards Amma's house. The tall man stopped the men behind them with a gesture, and he and the shorter one in the blue cloak strode forwards, halting only two paces from Amma's briggistanes.

Close to, Rannveig liked the look of them even less. The tall man was a wild Viking, with a hard, contemptuous look in his eye, and the shorter one had a long scar down one cheek that wrinkled his eyelid upwards into a puckered shape, and turned his eyeball white. Looking at them, she remembered Eilífr's description. These were Arisson's two friends, and they did not look to have come in peace. Her heart was cold within her, but she was not going to show how afraid she was. She let go of Fasti's hand, and stepped forward, head high.

'Welcome, strangers.' Hospitality was her duty. 'May I invite you up to our house for a glass of ale, and something to eat?' She gestured towards Underhoull. 'My father's house is just on the brow of the hill.' She swung her hand out towards the cluster of houses around Lund. 'Or perhaps you are seeking Nikolas of Lund? He himself is away in Skaillvarg, but his son will receive you. His house is over the hill, there.'

The men exchanged glances, calculating. Rannveig wished she had sent the children running for the house, while there had still been time. Then the tall Viking spoke, with an edge in his voice that sent the cold sweat running down her back. 'We have not yet decided who it is we are seeking. We have come to talk of the death of a friend.' He bent down to Fasti, with a smile that was hard as steel. 'You, boy, are you old enough to dream of voyaging across the waters?' He reached out a hand, and before Rannveig could move, he had caught the boy in a hard grasp and pulled him forwards. 'Why don't you go down and look at our ship?'

Rannveig thrust herself forwards against the Viking's bar-tight arm, pushing Fasti behind her. Out of the corner of her eye she could see Amma backing Fjorleif towards the doorway of her house. 'He is too young to go to sea yet. He is only seven.'

The tall Viking glared at her. He had half-raised his hand to sweep her out of the way when there was a shout from above, and Faider came striding down the hill with Sótr, their man-of-all-work, at his shoulder. He had not stopped to buckle on a sword, or pick up a knife; he had come straight from the workshop, his leather apron damp and smeared with clibber-dust. His voice rang out on the still air. 'Greetings, friends.'

The two men turned to watch him coming down the path. Their men did not move from their place, but came slightly together, squaring their shoulders. Rannveig pushed Fasti back behind her, and tugged him to the corner of the house. 'You and Fjörleif run up to our house, to Lína, and do whatever she tells you.' He jutted a mutinous lip at her. 'Now,' Rannveig ordered, and he looked at her face, and obeyed. She watched them go, filled with relief, then turned back to the men, and Faider, strong and determined in front of them.

'How may we serve you, strangers? I am Reifr of Underhoull.'

The scarred man answered him. 'We've come to enquire into the death of a friend of ours, Aldúlfr Arisson. We're told he died in the broch up there, of a knife wound, and was buried in your kirkyard.'

'We want to know,' the tall man added, 'what progress your Ting has made in finding his killer.'

'For that,' Faider said, 'your business is with Nikolas of Lund, the leader of our Ting. Nobody has been taken for his killer. There was a trial by bier-right before we buried him with all honours.'

The tall Viking snorted contemptuously. 'A bier-right - threats to frighten children! It seems you do not try hard to keep the law in this island.'

'If there has been no killer taken,' the scarred man said softly, 'then his family is due compensation for their loss. He stepped forward suddenly, the blue eye and the white one staring boldly into Faider's. 'Whether it comes from your community, who has failed to do him justice – '

The Viking stepped forward too. 'Or from you, since he died on your land.'

Rannveig could feel how much will-power was holding Faider still, confronting them. He was a peaceable man, fond of a drink with his friends, of telling stories over a good fire; he was out of his league with these two fighters, but pride would not let him retreat. 'I'll take you to Nikolas of Lund, who will tell you what was done to find out the man's identity, and search for the killer. As to compensation for his death, you must discuss that with him.'

'He was the king's man,' the scarred man said. 'The king will decide what he will accept, whether money or blood, once we have taken him all the facts.' He gestured towards Nikolas's house. 'Lead us, then, Reifr of Underhoull.'

ᚠᚠᚠᚠᚠ

Rannveig and her sisters waited anxiously all that morning for Faider to return. The sun was near its highest when Rannveig could bear it no more, and caught up her cloak. 'I'll go over to Lund and find out what's happening.' She looked around her. 'Where are the children?'

'At the beach,' Manga said. She pointed down to the curve of rock below Amma's house. 'Just behind where the strangers' knarr is pulled up. Fasti's fascinated by it. I saw him earlier, asking the sailors a dozen questions.'

'If you see the leaders coming back before I return, then go down and get him back to the house,' Rannveig said. 'I don't trust them.'

She strode over the hill, skirts kirtled up to her knees, jumping impatiently over the little burns. When she reached the brow of the hill, she saw others heading towards Lund: Father Jóhann pacing up from the church, hands behind his back, as if deep in thought; Jakob of Norwick, on his black pony, just coming past the Bordastubble stone, and his two sons with him; and surely that was Thórfastr of Vigga and his son, Halfthór, striding over the hill - their red hair was unmistakable. Just at the door of Lund was someone in a bright blue cloak: Arni of Baliasta. Rannveig felt a cold fear clutch at her heart. Young Nikolas had called the men of the Ting, as if there was a weighty decision to be taken, which he did not dare take alone. Surely, oh surely, they would never allow them to claim Faider as blood price for the man who had died in the broch. These were their neighbours, their friends ...

Young Nikolas was waiting at the front door of Lund, as if to greet each man as he arrived. Rannveig slipped around to the back of

97

the house. The women would be preparing a special meal in honour of these representatives of King Eystein. In the annexe, Kristin was delivering a flood of instructions: broth to be boiled, the sheep that had just been killed to be cooked in it, flat bread to be baked. Maria and her other daughter-in-law were scurrying round fetching flour, and boards for kneading the bread on; Geira was supervising the men tipping the pieces of sheep into the cauldron. She saw Rannveig, and her sulky face lightened. 'Look, Midder, here is Rannveig come to give us a hand.'

Kristin came to hug her. 'My thanks, dear child. We need all the hands we can get, with these two men arriving on us like this, without warning, and representing the Kings too, and Nikolas calling all the neighbours to meet them – all very well for him to say he knows I can cope, but a suitable feast in their honour can't be laid on just like that, as you well know.'

It was obvious that nobody had told her why they had been summoned. Rannveig set her cloak aside, rolled up her sleeves, and went to join Geira. 'Where have they taken Faider?' she whispered.

Geira tilted her head towards the hall. 'They're all in there. Once this broth is boiling, I'll take you around the side – we can listen at the other door.'

It seemed an age to Rannveig, stirring with the long-handled ladle, before the scum began to rise to the surface at last, but as one of the maids finished shaping her last piece of dough, Geira called her over to scoop the froth off and drew Rannveig out of the door and around the side of the house. 'Here,' she breathed. She eased the door open, and they heard a babble of voices, disagreeing.

'There is no proof,' said young Nikolas, over them, 'that Reifr of Underhoull was involved in the death of your friend Aldúlfr Arisson. The only footsteps that were found near the body did not match his.'

The tall Viking answered. 'He is the land-holder, the nearest house. Why would Aldúlfr have gone to the broch, if not to meet him?'

Rannveig knew the answer to that. Involuntarily she put her hand to the door, as if to push it open. Geira grasped her wrist and pulled her back. Their eyes met.

'Don't!' Geira begged. 'Don't hold me up to public shame by telling them all he was there to meet me.' Her hand was so tight around Rannveig's wrist that it felt as though she gripped the very bone. 'I beg you –'

'It is my father!' Rannveig breathed at her.

'I'll deny it!' Geira hissed. 'How could I have left this house full of people with nobody hearing? Who will my father believe, you or me?' Rannveig stared at her, biting her lip, and Geira pressed her advantage home. 'They will just say you would tell any tale to release him.'

'But he didn't kill that nobleman!'

'How do you know that? Maybe he did, after all – maybe he saw him in the broch, and challenged him, and Aldúlfr drew his sword, and they fought.'

'Then Faider would have said so.'

Geira's face was hard. 'Very well, then, have your say. But watch me first.' Her face smoothed; a faint frown came between her brows. 'Yes, I remember Aldúlfr Arisson – we met when I was a child, in Caithness, and he teased me. But I haven't seen him since – why should you say such a thing, Rannveig?' Her dark eyes met Rannveig's, wonderingly, then she turned away to face an imaginary Lawman. 'Unless she was meeting him herself...'

Rannveig's heart sank. Yes, Geira would be believed. 'Faider is innocent, Geira! Will you let them take him away from us – perhaps condemn him to death?'

'How should I know who killed him? It could be your father as easily as anyone else.'

'You're lying!' Rannveig was suddenly certain of it. 'You do know!'

'I tell you, I know nothing!' Geira flung Rannveig's wrist from her and whirled into the house.

Arguing with Geira. Rannveig had missed some of the discussion. Now Thórfastr of Vigga's voice rang out over the others. 'I wish to speak. Aldúlfr Arisson was not the first dead man at Underhoull. Patrekr of Baliasta died there last summer, in the house, with only my son, Lingormr, and Reifr of Underhoull present. My son was taken for Patrekr's murder, to the shame of our house, but he was convicted on the evidence of Reifr's daughter and the witness of the gallows run. He did not confess. Now, like Jakob, I begin to wonder. Only Reifr or my Lingormr could have killed Patrekr, but Lingormr was not here to kill this Arisson. Who is to say that there was not some underhand business between Reifr and Arisson that Patrekr found out, so that he had to be silenced? Then Arisson's death was a case of rogues falling out.'

Faider's voice rang out over him. 'What business would a clibber-carver have with a king's man?' Rannveig heard the scorn in his voice. 'I promise you, I've never been offered a commission to carve bowls for a king!'

'No honest business, that's for sure,' Thórfastr of Vigga retorted. 'Spying on your neighbour, maybe?'

Young Nikolas spoke slowly. 'But why would the king be interested in us? We are only simple farmers, his liegemen, not great nobles who might band together against him.'

'There are three kings in Norway,' Jakob of Norwick said. 'One might want to know what support he can count on, when the time came.'

A fist crashed on a table. The tall Viking spoke. 'That comes close to treason, old man!' The outburst of shouting that followed was silenced by the scarred man.

'A king's man died on this man's land. As for the story of this other death – '

'My son's death!' Arni of Baliasta cried out.

' – this must be sifted,' the scarred man finished. 'We will take this Reifr of Underhoull to King Eystein.'

Rannveig drew in a sharp breath. Her hand went up to her mouth.

'Arni of Baliasta, Jakob of Norwick, you are our Lawmen here, for our Alting!' Faider was trying to hide the desperation in his voice. 'I appeal to you for me to be tried here in Shetland.'

'We have the king's warrant to investigate,' the tall Viking said, 'and take what action we see fit.'

There was a sullen murmuring at this. Rannveig craned through the crack in the door, and saw the men crowding around a piece of parchment. 'This is the king's seal,' Jakob of Norwick conceded.

Afterwards, Rannveig did not remember running home over the hill, only the shocked faces of her sisters as she explained that they were taking Faider away. They prepared a bag for him, food for the journey, a spare tunic, sealskin rivlins, a warm cloak, with Rannveig thinking, thinking, all the time. If they were to ask a blood price for the dead nobleman, would their small hoard of silver be enough? Should she have tried telling the men that he had come to meet Geira? Yet if she hadn't been believed, it would have looked so much worse for Faider, as if she was lying to save him.

When they had done everything they could think of, they waited, standing together on the briggistanes. Faider came over the hill at last, walking with a heavier stride, shoulders bowed; Rannveig was reminded of the way he had walked up the hill after they had told him Midder was dead, as if his feet were too heavy to lift. Jakob of Norwick was at his side, his yellow cloak bright against the green hill. The tall Viking and the scarred man in the blue cloak walked with them, one on each side, like gaolers. They were heading for the ship, but they paused at the burn running down from the house. Rannveig could not hear the words, but the decisiveness of Jakob's tone carried on the still air. The tall Viking squared up belligerently, but the scarred man raised one hand to silence him, and nodded. Lína clutched Rannveig's hand.

'Oh, Ranka, how long do you think they will keep him?'

Rannveig shook her head. Her chest felt tight, as if she couldn't breathe properly. She put an arm around Káta. 'Where are the children?'

'Playing in the broch, I think. Shall I fetch them?'

Rannnveig nodded. 'They should say goodbye.'

Faider arrived at their briggistane at last. The strangers stood at the doorway, one on each side. Rannveig's mouth was too dry to ask questions. She could only look in silence, and follow as he came into the house and sat heavily on one of the benches.

'I am to go with them,' Faider said at last. 'They are on an expedition – they would not say where, but they are to join up with the main fleet in Leirvik, and one of their men died at sea. I am to take his place.'

'As a freeman, or as a thrall?'

Faider grimaced. 'Not a thrall exactly, I hope. I will work off the blood price.' He stretched out his hands, and Lína came to sit on one side of him, Manga on the other. 'You must be my good girls, and obey Rannveig.' He hugged them briefly, then stood up. 'I leave her in charge.' He walked to the door.

Rannveig looked despairingly at Jakob of Norwick. 'Is there nothing to be done?'

He shook his head, glancing at the men. 'They have King Eystein's warrant.'

'And the might of armed warriors behind it,' Rannveig thought. Their little community could not withstand a raiding party like this, if they chose to use their swords.

The scarred man slapped Faider on the back. 'Come, now, you'll be a cheery companion for us in this mood. We're giving you the chance to escape all these womenfolk and go a-viking. Doesn't your heart rise at the prospect?'

Faider gave him a contemptuous look. 'I can see you're not a family man.'

'We have everything we could think of ready for you, Faider,' Manga said.

'No, one last thing,' Rannveig said. She fumbled at the little silver cross round her neck. It had been her mother's, and she wore it always. 'Take Midder's cross, Faider, for protection while you are away from us.'

The tall Viking's hand came over hers and forced it down. 'No, woman, we'll have nothing of your lily-livered Christ on board. We are all Thór's men.'

'Come, then,' the scarred man said, 'the southbound tide won't wait for us.'

Faider looked around. 'Where are Káta, and the children?'

102

'She went to fetch them,' Rannveig said. She turned fiercely to the scarred man. 'Will you not let him say goodbye to all his family?'

The man turned his blind eye towards her, and shrugged. 'Can you hold the running tide for us?'

The tall Viking gestured downwards, and Faider picked up his bundle, wrapped in his cloak. His hand rested warm on Rannveig's shoulder. 'Give them my love.' He turned at the end of the flagged path to smile at them all. The girls watched the men diminish; a pause by Amma's house, then they were climbing into the boat, the crewmen pushed off, the oars dipped until the boat was clear of the rocks cradling the bay, and then the red sail was hoisted and bellied out in the wind.

Running footsteps sounded from the broch; Káta came stumbling along the path, pulling little Fjörleif with her. Her other hand was stretched towards the boat, and she was shouting, but the wind snatched the words away. Rannveig started towards her, alarmed. 'Where's Fasti?'

Fjörleif's face was tear-stained. 'He said I was to hide until the knarr left,' she wailed, 'then come and tell you. He said it would be an adventure.'

Rannveig felt her heart stop, then start again, bumping erratically. She forced herself to speak calmly. 'Fjörleif, where is Fasti?'

The little girl pointed to the ship. 'He hid under the cloaks.' Then she burst into tears again. 'I want him to come back,' she sobbed.

St Olav, save us – Rannveig crouched down to put her arm around the child. Below them, the ship altered course towards the open sea.

Chapter Ten

The Cult of Thór

Eilífr had never seen a city like Narbonne. Nidaros had been a city of wood, dominated by the great cathedral; this was almost too rich for his senses, with its pale stone castle, hung with tapestries from wall to wall, its twisted streets of brick and wood houses, where the upper gables leaned in over the street, so that gossips could pass an apple from one to the other, its jostling market filled with strange-smelling spices and fruits whose names he could not begin to guess. Then the warmth – to be able to walk out, even in the evening, in only his kirtle, with no need for cloak or leggings, was a new experience. In the afternoon, he stayed within the shelter of the castle walls, to keep out of the baking heat that beat down from the burnished sky, and rose from the dusty ground.

'But we didn't come for the city, or the warmth,' said Saebjörn. 'We have come this far unscathed, St Olav be praised! Now our prows should be pointed to the Holy Land, and our Earl delays us, whispering verses in a fair lady's ear.' He laughed. 'As we suspected he would.'

'She is fair indeed,' Eilífr agreed, 'and this game of courtly love suits our Earl well.'

'Oh, I grant you hair of gold and skin lily-white, and a quick wit besides.'

'But the lady Ermengard also has a husband, so there is no profit in wooing her.' Eilífr leaned forward against the ramparts, looking out over the spires of the city. 'And in so Christian a city, our Earl cannot just take the lady aboard and let love cry defiance at the world.'

'I have my own lady in mind,' Saebjörn said, 'as you have, and we won't get home to them with a chest of silver by hanging around here.' He turned his back on the river and tilted his face to the sky. 'I'm a northerner, suspicious of all this southern richness. Even the sky is too deep a blue for me. Yet it's strange too, being in a place where the gospel is so much more established than in Norway. There is a feeling at home, in spite of the miracles of our great St Magnus, that Christianity is as yet only laid over the pagan world that existed before.' He turned towards Eilífr. 'Do you feel that about Shetland, that the older people are still appeasing Odin, Loki, and Thór?'

'They say there are pockets of a Thór cult still,' Eilífr said. 'I know nothing about it. Nobody has ever approached me to join such foolishness.'

Saebjörn laid a hand on his shoulder. 'Hush, unless you wish to be a martyr. For the moment we have three kings, but what if they were to dwindle to only one, and that one a supporter of the old gods?'

Eilífr looked his surprise. 'Not King Inge, surely? I saw him first in the great cathedral in Trondehim.'

Saebjörn shook his head. 'King Inge will not make old bones. Nor do I mean King Sigurd. Didn't you notice that the Viking and his scarred friend wore Thór's hammer? King Eystein is the man I meant. And I wondered if perhaps that was what Aldúlfr Arisson was doing in your island – leading a meeting of Thór's men there, and establishing support for King Eystein. Could his death have been caused by a quarrel between them, or someone threatening to betray him?'

'I had not thought of that,' Eilífr said. He looked out over the city again, his eyes travelling blindly over the spires where the fork-tailed swallows swooped and circled. When he turned back to Saebjörn, his face was troubled. 'I was uneasy about my brother, Björn. He'd changed since I'd been away, he had more of a swagger to him, and there were several nights when he went out with a muttered excuse about meeting Hafthór of Vigga, and came back late, and smelling of ale. I didn't want to cause a row in front of my mother, but when I challenged him he said they'd simply sat at the fire, drinking. Now, I wonder ... might he be involved in such a cult?'

'His friend's name is suggestive. Hafthór. What's his family?'

'His father is Thórfastr of Vigga. He's brother to Lingormr, who killed Patrekr. You remember, the man I was accused of killing.'

Saebjörn turned to face him, leaning his shoulder against the wall. 'Why did he kill him?'

Eilífr shrugged. He'd pushed the memory away from him. 'I don't know if he ever said. Patrekr used to order him around – oh, even when we were boys, Patrekr used to throw his weight around, but this last six months he seemed to lean on Lingormr more, somehow, as if he just had to order, and Lingormr would jump to his bidding.'

'And this Patrekr, was his family Christian?'

Eilífr nodded. 'Arni of Baliasta joined with Nikolas of Lund to build our church. Patrekr himself, though, well, I think his eye was on the best profit.'

'So if he'd found out that Lingormr was part of a Thór cult, he might use it as a threat over him, to make him his errand-boy, rather than declaring it to your priest?'

'He would have indeed.' Eilífr grimaced, remembering Patrekr. 'You think he threatened once too often, and Lingormr took the chance of my quarrel with him to silence him, hoping that I'd be blamed?'

'You knew them. Do you think so?'

Slowly, Eilífr nodded. 'Yes.' He turned with a gesture of impatience. 'Oh, I wish we were on our way, and going home.'

ᚠᚠᚠᚠᚠ

Lund, Unst.
Skorpla, the second month of summer, 1151

Rannveig had had no heart to celebrate the summer blot at the start of Gaukmanudur, but she and her sisters went to the great bonfire at Lund all the same, and were a little comforted by Jakob of Norwick reminding them that this festival was for victory, and good luck on journeys; they could send their share of the luck to their father and Fasti – for all Unst had heard by now that their little brother had hidden himself on the ship. Rannveig had hoped that they would set him down at the first possible house on their way, for why would they want a seven-year old with them? As the days passed, and there was no word from Norwick, or Baliasta, then she knew she had hoped in vain. Faider being with him was her only comfort.

Nikolas of Lund had come round the very day he'd returned from Skaillvarg, his genial face grey and drawn into regretful lines. He folded her in a warm embrace, and for the first time since Faider had been taken she found herself crying. He harrumphed above her, and patted her shoulder, until she sniffed and rubbed a hand over her eyes. 'Oh, Nikolas, do you think they'll ever let him come home?'

'If only I'd been there. I'd never have permitted them to take him.' He patted her shoulder again. 'Now, don't fret, my dear. I'll do my best for him. I'll send to King Eystein in Norway, and offer to stand surety for a blood-price. In the meantime, how are you all managing? Can I send over a couple of thralls to help you with the voar work?'

They were glad of them, for it was the hardest time to be without Faider. Sótr, their man-of-all-work, took over hacking bowl shapes from the clibber on the hill, with one of Nikolas' men to help him, while Lína, Káta and Manga carved in the workshop. Rannveig and Nikolas' other man hauled seaweed from the beach to lay on the fields, between the rows of bere and pease, kishie-load after kishie-load on aching backs. It meant more mouths to feed, so that their store of food dwindled faster, and she was half-sorry, half glad when the field work was over, and they returned to their duties at Lund.

The oil was drawing up into the banks now, and it was time to cast their peats, for next winter's fuel. Rannveig was just wondering if she could ask Nikolas for a loan of his men again when Björn knocked diffidently at their door. 'I wondered,' he said, eyes downcast and cheeks reddening, 'if maybe you needed a hand with casting your peats.'

Rannveig could have hugged him. 'Oh, Björn! And you have your own to cast as well, with Eilífr gone. Will you really have time?'

He nodded. 'Ours are done. I'll come tomorrow.'

They arrived the very next day, he and his friend Hafthór of Vigga, ignoring the coolness between their families to help them when they needed it. They spent the day up on the hill, cutting blocks of the glistening black moor and throwing them out over the heather moor to dry, and came down as the sun began to slide behind the hills. Rannveig laid out the best feast she could provide at this end of the year: the last of the salted fish in a sauce flavoured with the first sorrel, dried mutton, a new cheese. They ate heartily and went away with an odd air of relief, as if they'd paid a debt. Rannveig puzzled over that, but could find no explanation.

Now all was going well. She and her sisters had got the peats raised, and the weather had been kind, with the days dawning bright, the sky palest blue fretted with clouds, and the sun sinking in a rose glow that promised another fine day tomorrow. The grass was white with daisies and lady-smock, and they'd been able to lay out all the house rugs, and burn the old heather bedding. The onions were well above ground, and the bere was a rich green rectangle. The lambs were frisking in mad groups, tails waggling; the cows and calves had been brought out into the fields, and grazed peaceably on their tethers. The burn was thick with the sword leaves and yellow flowers of flag-iris, and the fork-tailed tirricks swooped and dived above the blue water, and chittered on the beach. Soon it would be the solstice.

She and Manga were bent double, weeding between the rows of pease. It was hard, hot work, bent double under the sun. To her silent surprise, Nikolas the younger of Lund had come to help them, working down the row next to hers. 'Faider said to tell you that we'll send the two thralls again come harvest time, if your father's not home.' He prodded the soil with one foot, looking away from her. 'I wish Faider had been there, when your father was taken. They would have listened to him.'

'They had the king's warrant,' Rannveig said. 'You couldn't have argued against that.'

'If only they'd listened to me! It didn't make sense that your father should have killed him. And I told them of the other footprint, but they weren't interested.' His voice was bitter. 'They had a man to blame, and they took him.'

Suddenly, Rannveig liked him. 'Thank you for trying,' she said.

He dismissed that with a wave of his hand. 'And we hope you'll come to our solstice feast.' He saw the refusal in her face. 'For your sisters' sake, to cheer you all up.'

Rannveig was hesitating over that when Nikolas stood up, looking out to sea. 'A sail!' She stood up, her heart beating wildly. Nikolas shaded his eyes with his hand.

'Jakob of Norwick, back from Orkney.' He turned to Rannveig. 'He could have news of your father. Will I go and find out?'

'Oh, yes, yes!' Rannveig said. Nikolas nodded, and set off at a run towards Lund.

Rannveig watched the sail grow in size, then forced herself to keep working down the row, pulling up the arvie between the small plants, and thrusting the docken stems they'd dried over winter to hold them up. Now she could see the rowers, the steersman. News at last! Oh, how fervently she hoped so. As the boat came into the arms of the bay, the sail was lowered. She would do just one row more, then go and wash her hands.

The earth was soft here; she soon reached the place where the Nikolas had been working, and found his footsteps between the rows.

She drew in her breath. There, in front of her, was the foot she had been searching for, the foot she had seen again on a skekkler at Yule.

ᚠᚠᚠᚠᚠ

The footprint at last! Rannveig stared at the ground. The boot she'd been searching for belonged to Nikolas of Lund. And yet ... and yet ... she remembered how he had tried to find out about the killing. It was he who'd suggested taking the imprint of the foot. Surely if he'd known it was his own, he wouldn't have done that. It didn't make sense... unless ... had Arisson been killed by Geira, after all? They all lived in the same house. Had she taken her brother's boots to go and meet her lover? After all, she was Nikolas of Lund's daughter, with no need of working boots to go in the fields. It could well be that she had nothing suitable for crossing the hill on a dewy night. But then, if she had been the only one there, who had scuttled the boat?

112

Rannveig sat down on the dyke that bounded their rigs, looking out over the dancing water of Lunda Wick. The sun shone on the side of their little kirk. Nikolas of Lund had been the driving force behind its building; she remembered holding Midder's hand, and watching the men moving on the pale wood scaffolding. One of the window lintels was carved with a fish. She had traced it out with her finger, and Midder had told her that it was very old, from the time of the first monks who had brought Christ's gospel to Shetland. Rannveig closed her eyes and prayed to St Olav to help her. If she could find the real killer, then Faider would be released from King Eystein's galley. He would come home, and Fasti with him, and they would be a family again. Their faces haunted her: Faider, tired from rowing, treated as a thrall after years of being a freeman, and little Fasti, cold, frightened, hiding in the boat as a battle raged on shore. She had forbidden her sisters to talk any more of storms at sea, or attack from other ships, and she tried not to let herself imagine them, but her dreams were filled with great snatching waves.

She had to think. She knew a part of the story: Aldulfr Arisson had used Geira to find out all the gossip of the island, the news of the Ting. He'd reported it back to King Eystein, the oldest and least secure of the three kings in Nidaros. Geira had met Arisson that night in the broch, and they had quarrelled. Geira had said that she was pregnant, and begged Arisson to take her with him, and he'd refused. Their quarrel had been physical enough to break Geira's string of beads; she could have drawn his dagger from his belt and killed him with it. He wouldn't have been on his guard with her, as he would with a man. Rannveig remembered her belief that Geira knew more than she was willing to admit. If Geira had killed him then, was her brother Nikolas covering up for her? Or had he heard her leaving the house and followed her, heard her pleading with Arisson and killed him in defence of his sister's honour?

And where did the cult of Thór come in? The dead man had been a follower of the old gods, for he wore a Thór's hammer, and his friends, as they'd taken Faider, wouldn't allow her silver cross aboard their vessel. He could have been meeting with others, for the old

113

religion remained still, even though Norway had been fully a Christian country since the reign of St Olav. Suddenly, the names took on a new significance for Rannveig. Halfthór of Vigga's father was Thórfastr. Was it possible they'd kept to the old religion, that they still practised it, here in Unst, as Amma had said?

Then there had been the events of last midsummer, the death of Patrekr of Baliasta in their house. That was how it had all started. Lingormr, Halfthór's brother, had been executed for his killing, and at the time she'd thought it had been because he'd had enough of the way Patrekr ordered him around. Now, Rannveig wondered about the reason for Patrekr's bullying attitude. Had he known something which he'd held over Lingormr's head – the Vigga family's allegience to the outlawed religion? Perhaps Patrekr had been killed to silence him.

She could not sit here on the hill any longer. She jumped to her feet and strode along the hill ridge towards Lund. There was a bustle around the door, with Jakob of Norwick in his blue cloak at the heart of it, and Nikolas of Lund beside him, hands flung up in disbelief. She quickened her stride, chest tight, as if a cold hand was gripping her heart. Oh, Faider, little Fasti ...

He was a kind man, Jakob of Norwick. He'd spoken up for Faider when King Eystein's men had said they'd take him away. He looked up now, saw her hurrying across the hill, and came to meet her, hands held out. 'Don't worry! I haven't come with bad news. On the contrary. Your father and brother are well. I spoke with them myself, in Orkney.'

A rush of joy flooded Rannveig's heart. She found herself crying, and brushed the tears away. 'You've seen them?'

'In Kirkwall.' He shook his head, disbelieving. 'There have been great doings down there. You know that the men who took your father were joining King Eystein's fleet – well, he was taking the chance of Earl Rögnvaldr's crusade to raid his lands. He sailed down to Orkney, with a large war party, but he found Harald Maddadarson was on a voyage to Caithness, so he followed him there, boarded his vessel and kidnapped him.'

Rannveig remembered the young man who'd stood at the Earl's side at the Ting a year ago, straight and silent, with a dark, ugly face. 'Kidnapped him?'

'He was taken completely by surprise. What could he do? So now, as his ransom, his part of Orkney belongs to King Eystein.' Jakob of Norwick chuckled. 'That'll raise a stour o' wind when Earl Rögnvaldr comes home.'

'But Faider?'

Jakob of Norwick patted her hand. 'In good time, my dear. The king brought Maddadarson to Kirkwall to seal his allegience in front of all the nobles there, and that's how I fell in with the fleet. Your father was well, and being treated kindly enough, not like a thrall, like any other freeman who'd joined the fleet of his own free will. As for your brother, well, your father was keen that I should bring him home with me, but the young imp refused.'

Jakob shook his head, remembering. Fasti had stood straight before him, dark head high, and insisted, 'I want to go to sea, and be a warrior.' The tall Viking who was in charge had laughed and tousled his hair.

'He's got spirit,' the Viking had said. 'Seven's old enough to leave the women, and learn about the men's world.' He'd sent Fasti back aboard the boat, and Jakob could do nothing, nor would the boy obey his father's orders to go home with him. Fasti was in a fair way to being spoiled as the ship's mascot, but he wouldn't tell that to his anxious sister.

'And is there any sign that they'll let Faider come home?' Rannveig asked.

Jakob shook his head. 'It won't be this summer, for King Eystein is off a-viking. I watched them sail south the next morning, bound for Scotland, maybe even the north of England too. He claimed it was to avenge the death of King Harald Sigardurson, but I doubt anyone believed that. No, he's consolidating his own position.'

'But at the end of the summer ...' Rannveig bit her lip. 'Jakob, if we gave King Eystein's men the real killer of Aldúlfr Arisson, they would set Faider free, would they not?'

115

Jakob spread his hands. 'It would seem justice. But ...' He gave her a keen look from under his busy eyebrows. 'Do you know who the killer was?'

Rannveig spread her hands. 'I have ideas ... nothing sure, as yet.' She glanced over at Lund house, at young Nikolas standing beside his father, with Geira at his shoulder, and bit her lip. 'Nothing that would be believed.'

He put a hand on her shoulder. 'Keep thinking. If ever you are sure, come to me. I'll do what I can to help.'

ᚠᚠᚠᚠᚠ

Tvimanudur, two months until winter 1151

Rannveig had stayed later than she'd meant at Hunsta. There had been a late-summer feerie running round the children, vomiting and fever. Fjörleif had been very ill for two days, but Rannveig and Manga had nursed her to recovery. Now Arni of Hunsta's grand-daughter had been taken suddenly with pains in the belly, and Arni himself had come to ask Rannveig to see what she could do for the child. It was only common sense, to keep her quiet, give her drinking water that had been boiled, and pile covers over her until the fever fought itself out, but little Birla was the family's darling, and Rannveig arrived at Hunsta to find them all in a state of panic. She shooed all but Birla's mother out of the chamber they'd put her in, forbade them to feed her any more, gave the child a very little of her poppy syrup to make her sleepy and got her to lie still while she told her a long story of how the hero Sigurdur killed the dragon Fafnir. At last the child fell asleep, and though her face was still flushed, her breathing was slowed. Rannveig waited until she was sure the vomiting was past, and the child sleeping naturally, then set out to make her way home. Arni had offered to walk with her, but she laughed at him, and gestured up at the sky.

116

'Arni, look at this moon! How can I get lost on the hill in this short distance? Stay you with your family, and don't let them feed the child anything except water tomorrow. Well, she may have an oatcake for supper, but no butter or cheese, mind! Just a plain oatcake, and definitely not before dusk, unless you want her to start vomiting again.'

He promised to make sure his wife and daughter obeyed, and waved her off with thanks.

The harvest moon hung in the sky, yellow as butter, slanted eyes laughing at her. Rannveig walked briskly along the narrow path between the hills of Hunsta and Hamarberg, enjoying the smell of the night air around her, the damp grass and honey heather, and the way the moon shone gold on the water, sharpening the black of the headlands. The moon dimmed the stars around her, but in the other half of the sky the sailor's star twinkled blue-white, and Odin's wagon hung above Underhoull. She came between the small waters and onto the main pathway that branched down past the Bordastubble Stone to Lund, and went onward to Underhoull and the houses past it.

A light sparked in the darkness to her left. She slowed her pace, looking and listening. A lit lantern perhaps, another traveller coming up from Lund. Rannveig felt her heart beating uncomfortably, and scolded herself for being stupid. What harm would come to her here from a lone walker, someone who'd stayed too long enjoying Nikolas' hospitality? It would be a neighbour she knew. All the same, she kept her feet soft, and moved more swiftly, so that she'd be already along the road to Underhoull when he came up to the fork. A horsegok came whirring up from under her feet, and made her start back, suppressing a cry. Suddenly she remembered Amma, on the night of the Christmas feast at Lund: *I saw lights at the Bordastubble Stone, last Winternights.*

She was moving, but the tiny gleam was not. As far as she could tell, it remained where she'd first seen it. She stopped to stare. It was not bright enough for a torch, and burned with a steady gleam; an oil lamp, perhaps, placed on the ground, or on a boulder. As she watched it winked into darkness, then glowed orange again, as if someone had crossed in front of it.

All her instincts told her to walk on, get away from there as swiftly as she could, home to the warmth of the peat fire, and the door closed against the dark. Her sisters would be getting anxious. Yet her reasoning mind told her that here might be a chance to find out more. She could find out at least if this was a cult of Thór, and who was involved. Yes, it was a slim chance that she would see anything that would solve the mystery of Arisson's death, but she had to take any chance that offered. She thought of Faider, pulling the heavy oar for the tall Viking and his scarred companion, and of little Fasti, exposed to cold, and storms, and battle, wishing he was home safe with his big sister to cuddle him, and took a deep breath. She would go and look.

It took an effort of will to turn and begin to walk, slowly, softly, towards the light. It kept blinking out, as if there were several people moving around it. Her feet were silent on the soft grass. Now she could hear soft voices, men's voices chanting. She paused for a moment, listening, but could not make out words.

Forwards, forwards, sliding each foot carefully. She remembered the game she and her sisters had played, where one turned her back while the others crept up to her. The trick was to move so slowly that the one you were creeping up on could not see you moving. She steadied her breathing. They were only a hundred paces away now. Surely this was close enough!

She crouched down so that her shape would be a boulder on the moonlit hill, and stared into the darkness. There were about seven or eight men moving around the Bordastubble. The light was set on a low stone, and they kept crossing it, so that it was hard to make out the number, but there were at least six of them, circling the stone, with the low chanting swelling and dying away again as the soft wind brought it to her. She couldn't make out the words, except for the name Thór, being repeated now over and over, gradually getting louder and quicker. Someone raised the lamp higher, and she saw that they were all wearing pointed hoods of some kind, made of skins, with the animal's back falling down behind them. Then the lamp was handed forward. It flamed from below on a monstrous face, crowned by ridged goat horns that were black as death against the red glow on the Bordastubble Stone.

Rannveig flinched back, catching the scream in her throat. The creature was taller than the others, white-faced, with short hair that glinted in the lamplight. Then her eyes made sense of what she saw. It was a head-dress, a helmet made of goatskin, like the others were wearing, except that this was a he-goat with those great, sharp horns. The chanting ended in a shout, and the lamp was lifted high, shining out over the hill. Rannveig sank her head into her knees. She hardly dared breathe as the silence lasted. The wind rustled the grasses beside her, and there was the smell of moss in her nostrils. Her heart was thudding. If they had seen her ... and then there was a jeering of laughter from below her, and the sound of a jug being uncorked. Ale splashed into a drinking horn.

She risked lifting her head. The lamp had been replaced on the stone, and the goat's head-dress with it, the shadow of the horns stretching up tall against the Bordastubble. One man was standing beside it, one hand on the stone, the other outstretched; they were serving him first. He, the man who had worn the goat head-dress, must be the leader of this cult. The flagon went round, then he raised his drinking horn. The moonlight glinted on silver bands at top and bottom. The toast travelled clearly across the hill: 'To Thór!'

She had to get closer. She thought she knew the voice, but she needed to see the face. While they were intent on their ale, they wouldn't be looking around them. She thought of Fasti and Faider and told herself that she could do it. Staying crouched, she shuffled forwards, step by step, hands on the wet earth to help her keep her balance. Now a platter was being handed round, and there was a soft blur of talk.

Forwards. Her skirt was trailing on the ground. She bundled it up into her lap, and felt the folds wet. Now the grasses rasped against her bare legs, but if she had to run for it she would be as well to have her skirt kilted up. She tucked it into her girdle. Her thighs were beginning to ache with the effort of shuffling forwards like this. She

119

leaned forward on her hands for a moment, trying to stretch the muscles. Surely she didn't need to go much further.

There was a burn running down between her and the Bordastubble. She could hear it trickling now, and make out the dark line cutting the hillside. She wouldn't be able to cross that, but the noise it made would mask her approach. Ten paces further.

Yes, she was starting to make out individuals now. That was Eilífr's brother Björn. Márgret of Vinstrick would be horrified to see her son at a gathering like this. Beside him was Hafthór of Vigga, and others of the same age, the young men of Unst.

They were standing in front of the man who had worn the goat mask. *Move*, she begged them silently. *Let me see his face*. Time seemed to stand still. There was only now, with her crouching there in the darkness, the burn running at her feet, and the smell of moss swirling upwards. They were moving now, but he was moving with them, she was going to lose her chance ... then, as he lifted the lamp to blow it out, she saw his face.

Her eyes were accustomed to the dark, and theirs were not. She rose quickly and began to hurry across the dark hill, towards home. The path would have been smoother, but soon she would be on their own ground, with dykes to hide behind. Her breathing was coming in great gasps, her heart hammering, but no shouts split the silence of the night. She had escaped... and she had seen him. Now she had the answer she needed.

Their leader was young Nikolas of Lund.

Chapter Eleven

A Murderer Unmasked

She lay awake that night, listening to Lína and the others girls breathing softly beside her, for they all slept together now in the main room of the house, in the warmth of the fire, and with Sótr in the annexe by the door. Her mind was in turmoil. She remembered Nikolas of Lund's many kindnesses, and didn't want to bring this upon him, yet if she didn't speak out, then Faider and Fasti would never come home.

The next morning she went to Lund.

Nikolas was busy about the sheepfold, where they were separating the lambs from the ewes. She asked if she could consult him, and he showed her into the hall, seated her by the fire, and pressed a beaker of blaand on her. That done, he sat by her side, and asked how he could help, his comfortable face drawn into concerned lines.

It was difficult to begin. She plaited her apron-skirt between her fingers, and could not look at him. 'I know who killed Aldúlfr Arisson.'

He rose abruptly at that, and began to pace the room, pausing to glance out of the window, to look back at her, then resuming his walk. His right hand tugged at his beard. 'Who?'

Rannveig bit her lip, then lifted her face to look straight at him. 'You killed him.'

He hadn't expected that. His brows shot together, his mouth hardened. She had forgotten that as well as their family friend he was a landowner, a trader, a man accustomed to driving a hard bargain. Suddenly the room was very quiet, with all the men busy outside among the bleating sheep. He looked at her as if she was a stranger. 'Well? I suppose you have a reason for this accusation.'

'For a start,' Rannveig said, 'he must have had a reason for being in our broch. I knew he wasn't visiting us, and Olav of Bordastubble wasn't a man to know a king's courtier. That left Thórfastr of Vigga, and you, here at Lund. If he'd been visiting either of you, he could have come openly to Lunda Wick, instead of hiding his boat in the geo below the broch. There was no harm in a visitor from Norway.

Even if you were engaged in something clandestine with him, you could have said he was a trading connection. So, I reasoned, he must have been meeting someone from one of your two households, unknown to the head of the household.'

Nikolas did not speak. Rannveig took a sip of the milk, and continued, her hands trembling. 'The children found a spun-glass bead in the grass. It came from Geira's necklace.'

He snorted contemptuously. 'A glass bead. It could have lain there for ten years.'

'She told me about their meetings.'

He turned away from her, and swung over to the window. There was a long silence.

'I think,' Rannveig said, 'that you already suspected something. Perhaps not. Perhaps you just woke, and heard the door closing, then looked out and saw her hurrying across the parks. She was wearing her brother's boots. I recognised the sole. I would have suspected him of the killing, except that he was the one who suggested I copied the footprint. He would never have done that if he'd known it was his. But you scoffed at the idea.'

'A boy's foolishness. I'm glad you're not throwing accusations at my son as well.'

Rannveig twisted her hands in her lap. 'I don't want to throw accusations at anyone. I'm sorry for Geira, and I don't want to shame her at the Ting. Arisson didn't love her. He was using her to get information about Shetland for King Eystein, to find out who might come onto his side if he made a move against Earl Rögnvaldr.'

'If he'd been making approaches to others, then it's strange nobody recognised him.'

'How could they admit to treason? But someone sent the word that brought his men here, the ones who took Faider. They already knew all about Arisson's death at the broch.' Rannveig paused, then lifted her head again. 'But I think he had another purpose for being in the isles. He was a follower of Thór, and led a group of Thór-worshippers here.' She looked up at Nikolas again. 'Several of the young men of the isles. I saw them at the Bordastubble last night.

Nikolas was their leader.'

His brow had darkened. 'In defiance of God's word, and against the king's decrees.'

'Yes,' Rannveig agreed. 'I think you would have known about it. You know everything that goes on here, you hear whispers. But you couldn't put a stop to it, within sight of your own church, without proclaiming your own son a part of it. And then, that night, you realised that Geira too was mixed up in something discreditable. You followed her, and heard what she said to Arisson, and how he dismissed her. You went into the broch and confronted him. You're a powerful man. Geira couldn't have killed Arisson with a clean stab to the heart like that, but you could have. You had reason enough; not only his undermining of the religion in the isles, but his treatment of your daughter. Geira ran away, and that's when Oskur began barking. I think you'd have put him in his boat and scuttled it if you'd had time, but you knew the dog would wake the household. You just had to leave the dead man there and get back here to Lund, where we'd come to get you. You scuttled the boat later. Fasti saw you, but he didn't see who it was.' She shook her head. 'Clothes, well, they aren't remembered, but those men who took Faider would have known Arisson's boat.'

'If I'd done this, would I have sent for the men of the isles to identify him? Would I have held the ordeal by bier-right?'

'You knew who he was, and that King Eystein would look for him. If you'd admitted to his identity, the Ting would have had to investigate, and then Geira's connection with him and the Thór-cult might be made public. You couldn't risk that. You had to gamble that Thór-worshippers wouldn't name him, nor would Geira.'

'And the ordeal?'

'If King Eystein sent someone to investigate, you'd done something to try and trace his killer. You knew everyone but you could honestly swear their innocence of his death.'

He sat down beside her and leaned towards her, laying one hand over hers. 'Rannveig, I helped build the church on the headland there. With my own hands, I hewed timber and hauled stones. You know that. I remember you, as a little girl, standing beside your mother, watching. Do you think I would stand there before God and swear falsely?'

'No,' Rannveig said. 'You wouldn't do that.'

He leaned back from her. 'Well, then.'

'You didn't swear,' Rannveig said. 'You stood beside the body and invited the others to come up. Arni of Baliasta, Jakob of Norwick, all of them. I saw how uneasy the young Thór-worshippers were. They all swore, but you didn't.' She turned to him, eyes bright with tears. 'Nikolas, I don't want to have to tell any of this! I just want Faider home, and Fasti, safe where he belongs, instead of at sea with those raiders. Can't you do anything to bring them home to us?'

Nikolas spread his hands. 'What could I do?'

'You could go to his kin in Norway and make a clean tale of it. You could offer a blood price.'

He shook his head. 'I've learned something by this, Rannveig. Geira needs a husband, so I'm going to marry her off as soon as possible. Who'd take her if this tale was published abroad? Not that I'm admitting there's any truth to it, mind! But just the rumour would be enough. One word from you or one of your sisters - '

'My sisters know nothing of this.'

There was another long silence. His face was grim, as if he was thinking something through. 'Voyaging time's not over yet. If I was to go to Norway, to his kin, would that content you? I don't need to mention Geira. I could say I felt responsible, as the landowner for this area of Unst. I'll offer them a blood price.' He looked at her from under his brows. 'It'll be a heavy one. If I do this, will you keep silence?'

She nodded.

He held out his hand, as if they were agreeing the price of a beast. His face was back to its genial lines, but there was a hard shrewdness in his eyes that made her uneasy. 'Silence, for your father and Fasti's return.'

She laid her hand in his. 'Silence.'

126

ᚠᚠᚠᚠᚠ

It was two evenings later. Sótr had laid rabbit snares on the rocky headland between their bay and Lunda Wick, and she'd come to see if he'd had any luck, so that they could have roasted rabbit for supper. She'd found two in the snare, and was just picking her way downwards in the dusk, a dead rabbit dangling from each hand, when there was a footstep behind her. Two hands shoved her. She was catapulted forwards, down the steep slope, tumbling right over first, limbs flailing, then landing on her back with a thud that knocked the breath out of her. She rolled downwards from there, the rocks jabbing into her, her hands scrabbling for a hold among the slippery grass that tore her skin as it slipped through her fingers. The sea mouthed the rocks below.

It was her skirt that saved her, catching in the gap between two rocks. One moment she was falling, then the next she was suspended, hands grasping out into air, with the dark rocks thirty feet below. Her legs and belly were safe on the grassy slope. If she had time she could extricate herself, but she was afraid that she wouldn't be given the chance. She could feel the strong hands on her back, like a bruise. She raised her spinning head and called for help, a breathless sound at first, then with all the force her gasping lungs could manage. Silence, Nikolas of Lund had said, and this was how he intended to make sure she kept silence. Was that a footstep above her? She thought the turf under her cheek quivered, and lifted her head to call again, and again. If they did not hear her now, there was no hope. She could feel his heavy tread moving down the hill towards her. He would throw her down, and say she'd been over-wrought from missing her father, make up a story of what she'd said to him when she'd come to seek him at Lund. They'd bury her in a suicide's grave.

The thought made her angry, and the anger gave her strength. She drew her hands back under her and used them to prise herself up from the ground. She tried to back away from the fall before her, but her skirt was caught fast, twisted round her legs, and she could barely turn within it. She could hear his footsteps now, coming faster towards her in the dimming light. She yelled again, and this time a gold square of light sprang up at Underhoull as someone opened the door. He was ten paces from her, face darkened into a stranger's, hands outstretched towards her. The words he'd use echoed in her head: *I tried to stop her, but I was too late ...*

A voice reached out to her, Manga, calling her name. Then Nikolas was on her in a rush, trying to roll her over. She screamed again, and heard Manga's answering cry. His grasping hands tightened on her, then loosed again; he felt for his knife, and went for her skirt with a long slash. The fabric tore, and she felt herself slide. Desperately, she caught at his ankles and pushed with all her strength. She felt him overbalance, arms letting go of her to clutch the air, and then with a sickening thud he fell. It seemed to her, watching, as if everything happened slowly: he staggered backwards, and then he was tumbling as she had tumbled, body tossed like a child's toy down the slope. She winced from the impact as he was flung onto the rocks. He writhed there for a moment, howling in pain. The hungry sea came up over him, and when the wave retreated again he was lying still. Only his arms dragged backwards with the tide's pull.

They were running now, Manga and Lína, with Sótr overtaking them. They must have seen Nikolas fall, for Sótr went straight to the beach, and threaded his way between the rocks to catch at Nikolas and pull him clear, while her sisters came to her, climbing carefully up the slope. She clutched Lína's hand, shuddering, while Manga freed her skirt. They helped her up and walked with her back to the house. There she sat and clutched a beaker of ale with shaking hands while they fussed around her. 'But what happened?' Manga asked at last.

She'd had time to think of her answer. She'd promised Nikolas silence, and she would keep her word. 'I slipped on the grass, and tumbled right down. Luckily my skirt caught on those rocks, but when Nikolas came to help me, then he slipped.'

She repeated the story to Jakob of Baliasta the next day. She had slept badly, dreaming of finding herself falling and gasping awake, and when she rose in the morning she was stiff and sore, with darkening bruises all over. Jakob looked at her with concern. 'You're not hurt?'

She shook her head. 'I was fortunate.'

Jakob shook his head. 'Ah, he was a good man, Nikolas of Lund, a great part of our community.' He gave her a sharp look from under his bushy brows, and she wondered if he guessed more than she had said. 'You'll need to come and explain what happened at the Ting.' He rose. 'Don't worry, you won't be asked many questions. It's straightforward enough. You fell, he came to help you, and slipped on the evening dew. We'll meet tomorrow afternoon.'

It took her back to where it had all begun, at the Alting, with the bright banners waving against the summer sky, and the green grass running down from the red-bricked church to the loch. Then, she had had Faider to give her courage, and Eilífr's life to fight for. Now she was standing, waiting, with Lína and Káta on one side of her, and Fjörleif between her and Manga, hands clasped. The hairst wind was still warm, blowing her hair. The hill was patched with dark orange now, the bog asphodel brightening as it withered. The pease had been harvested, and the bere, but the short grass was still summer green, with the longer stems bleached to pale gold. The fork-tailed tirricks had gone, and the comical puffins with their frantic wing-beats, but the solan geese still soared and dived in the sound, white wings spread into a cross. On the shore, the seaweed draped orange locks over each stone.

They were coming now. She drew back to let them pass: Father Jóhann leading, then Jakob of Norwick, Arni of Baliasta, and young Nikolas of Lund, dressed in black. He was followed by all the other freemen of the region. If Faider had been here, he would have walked with them. She waited outside the broch, watching the glinting water, listening to the murmur of voices from within the great stone circle, and prayed for St Olav to grant her the strength to lie.

Her summons came at last. Jakob of Norwick came to call her, and laid his hand on her shoulder, propelling her into the circle.

'Speak out, Rannveig Márgretsdottir.'

Rannveig felt her breath coming short. It should have been less frightening than the Ting, not a league from her own house, and with every face someone she had known from her childhood, but somehow the very familiarity made it worse. The stone walls pressed in on her, and the curious faces round her made her heart thump. She closed her hand around her pouch, and felt the leather outline of the footprint she had copied. Suddenly she wondered if she was doing the right thing. If she told all, would they send word to Norway that Arisson's killer was dead, and bring Faider and Fasti home?

'Speak, Rannveig Márgretsdottir,' Jakob repeated.

For a moment she imagined herself saying it. 'Nikolas of Lund killed Arisson, and he tried to kill me.' They would not believe her; why should they? She would need to explain the whole story, Geira's love for Arisson, the Thór-cult and young Nikolas's part in it, and even if they believed her she couldn't be sure it would bring Faider back. She moistened her lips. Her voice did not sound like her own. 'I went to get rabbits from our snares, and I slipped. There was dew on the grass. Nikolas came to help me, and he fell. I was fortunate – my skirt caught in the rocks, and that saved me.' She had meant to look straight around her, but at the last minute she could not do it, and let her eyes fall. It was over.

ᚠᚠᚠᚠᚠ

They gave Nikolas of Lund a Christian burial in the kirk he had sponsored, and raised a stone cross over him. Two days after the funeral, young Nikolas came to Underhoull. His shadow blotted out the light as she worked in the booth behind the house, and she jumped, heart in her throat.

He had aged, she thought, since the loss of his father. His face had lost the boyish look, become graver. He raised a hand reassuringly.

'There are six weeks yet to Winternights. There's word that King Eystein is back in Orkney now. I'm going down to meet with him, to give allegience and consolidate my position there.' He gave her a long look. 'I'll speak to him of your father. I can make no promises, but if he'll accept a blood-price, then it'll be paid, and I'll bring him home.' He nodded at her, and swung away.

ᚠᚠᚠᚠᚠ

Gormanudur, slaughter month, 1151

He was away for five long weeks. As they did the last work outside, Rannveig found herself watching the horizon for the ochre sail. They were pulling up the last of the dried pea-stalks for winter bedding when Káta turned with a cry, and pointed. 'It's young Nikolas of Lund back, surely it is!'

Manga's hand slid into Rannveig's, and gripped hard. Beside her, Lína's breathing rattled in her throat; Fjörleif shrieked and dropped her bundle of pease helms to clap her hands.

'Maybe he's brought Fasti home!' She began to run down the hill, gold plaits flying behind her. 'Fasti, Fasti!'

By the time the blind prow had crunched on the pebbles of their beach, they were all there, waiting, silent, scanning the faces of the oarsmen. Rannveig was afraid to hope, seeing only Nikolas' men, then she found Faider at last, second from the end, turning to smile at them as he backed his oar. A rush of joy swept through her. For a moment she thought she might faint. Fasti was beside him, stretching up to look over the side, and he was waving. They were both safe.

One of Nikolas' men swung Fasti ashore, and he charged up the beach, shouting as he ran: 'Ranka, I've been in a battle!'

She lifted him and swung him round, wanting never to let him go, but he was already squirming in her arms. 'I'm too big to be lifted. Fjörleif, I was in a battle – just wait till I tell you all about it.'

Rannveig set him down and ran to Faider. He was looking well, almost younger, for he'd lost weight, and his face and arms were tanned with the summer sun glancing from the sea, but there were new lines between his brows and at the corners of his mouth, and a sprinkling of grey in his dark hair. He put an arm around her. 'Well, Ranka, I hear it was you who won me my freedom.'

She shook her head, and hugged him. 'Oh, Faider, we've missed you so much. St Olav be praised that you're home at last.'

ᚠᚠᚠᚠᚠ

Haustmanudur, harvest month, a year later

It had taken them time to adjust to being home. Faider had seemed cheerful enough, walking round the croft and praising all they'd done while he was away, or telling his new stories to Olav of Bordastubble over the hnefatafl board. They'd joined up with King Eystein's fleet in Leirvik: 'A great fleet of ships, that filled the whole bay,' Faider told them. They'd sailed and rowed to Orkney first, as Jakob of Norwick had reported, then to Thurso bay, where they'd taken Harald Maddadarson. 'Then it was on to Scotland. King David's son, Henry, had just died and the old king was too lost in mourning him to make a proper defence, so we raided several towns there. We went as far south as Hartlepool, and made a fine profit there.' He put an arm round Lína. 'You girls will have good dowries now. I'll accept nothing less than an Earl's son for you.'

Rannveig could see that Fasti had been thoroughly spoiled on the voyage. It took three weeks of determined firmness before he would obey her again, and although he didn't seem to be troubled by what he'd seen, the stories he told her gave Fjörleif nightmares, until Rannveig had to forbid him telling her any more.

She didn't tell Faider how Arisson had died, and he didn't ask. Perhaps she might tell Saebjörn when he returned – if he returned. Stories of Earl Rögnvaldr's journeys had filtered back with travellers. He'd lingered in Narbonne with the Lady Ermergard, and written her many fine poems; they'd sacked a castle in Galicia, and taken chests of plunder, but not as much as they could have, because Eindreidi the

Young had made a private bargain with the castle's lord to spare his life in exchange for the best of his valuables; they'd sailed on past Gibraltar, and taken a dromond as big as an island, but fired it with the gold still hidden inside, so that a stream of molted metal poured into the water. They'd reached the Holy Land, and visited all the sacred places there, then gone on to Constantinople, where the Emperor had invited them to join his bodyguard. They'd returned overland to Rome, where Earl Rögnvaldr had knelt to the Holy Father himself. But when Lína questioned eagerly if all his men were well, the pedler telling the tales shrugged his shoulders. 'I can't tell you that. So many adventures, there are bound to be some casulties. There was disease at Acre, and the poet Thórbjörn died of it. Others too, I suppose. Who can say?'

Lína didn't speak of that later, as Rannveig had expected, but from that news she seemed to shut in on herself, and her rose skin paled to the white of the sea-foam. If she did not brighten when next spring came, Rannveig told herself, then she must talk to Faider, though it was hard to see what could be done. As for herself, she hardly dared hope, yet she would not give up waiting for him. The Earl led a charmed life, and Rome was a long way away. Saebjörn's brooches shone on her shoulders at Yule, and again at the spring equinox blót, the summer blót, the solstice bonfire. She would wear them once more this year, at Winternights, and then put them away until spring, when she might hope again that he'd come soon.

Rannveig was carving a platter in the booth when she looked up to see a sail coming around the headland to the south. It was a small ship, not much larger than their own faerling, with only four oars. It came past Nikolas' beach to slip into their own bay. Her heart thumped, and her breath caught in her throat. Slowly, she rose, shielding her hand with her eyes against the low sun. The boat slid to the shore, and the first two men jumped out. Her hand let her knife fall onto the bench; her breath stilled, disbelieving. They were far off, but surely, surely, she knew Eilífr's dark head, and Saebjörn's proud walk. They had come! She sprang up and stumbled into the house. 'Lína, Lína, come quickly!' She caught her sister's hand. 'I'm afraid to believe it – look there!'

Lína gave a startled cry, then clung to her. 'It is, it *is*! He's come home at last.' They were half way up the hill now, climbing steadily, eyes fixed on the house. Lína let go of Rannveig's hand and began to run. Eilífr caught her in his arms and swung her up and around, and their laughter filled the air. Rannveig came forward to meet Saebjörn, eyes fixed on his.

'Do I get a welcome too?' he asked, and she nodded, smiling, and ran forward into his arms. They tightened around her; he kissed her soundly. Then there was a jostling in the doorway, and a confusion of people around, Káta bidding the strangers welcome, and Manga fetching the ale, and Faider swinging the door open.

'We came home on a merchant ship,' Eilífr said, his arm round Lína, 'all the Earl's company who were left, and a fine show we made. But there are arguments in Orkney, and so we left the Earl to knock heads together, and made our best speed home.'

Saebjörn turned his head to gaze at the grazing cattle, the neat pattern of fields running down to the calm voe, the boats drawn up on the beach. His arm tightened around Rannveig's waist. 'It's very different from Orkney, but I could feel it to be home. You'd want to be near your family, I think.'

She nodded, joy rising within her. She'd been prepared, of course, to go where fortune took her, but if he would feel at home here, so much the better. 'We could see if Jodis of Baila might consider giving us land to start with.'

'I have plenty to keep us busy here,' Faider said, 'with Amma's land and our own. Lína will be off to Vinstrick as fast as Eilífr can take her there, and as for Káta and Manga, well, who knows where they'll end up.'

'There's no hurry for me,' Manga said. 'What would you all do without me?'

'And I'm going to go to sea!' Fasti declared. 'I'm not going to be a farmer, but a shipmaster, like you.' He gave Saebjörn a pleading look. 'Do you think the Earl would take me on for his next voyage?'

134

Saebjörn's hand tightened on Rannveig's. 'If you work at your books, and listen to what the priest teaches you. The Earl is a poet, remember. He wants men who can think and talk as well as they can fight. If you do well, then when you're twelve, I'll take you down to Orkney and ask him for a place for you – but I can make no promises, mind.'

Fasti whooped, and picked up Oskur's front paws to dance round the yaird with him. 'I'm going to sea, I'm going to sea!'

'Well,' Faider said, 'if that's all settled, when are you going to wed?'

Rannveig felt herself blushing. Saebjörn's hand moved up her back and settled warmly on her shoulder. 'It's but a month to Winternights. Would that give you time enough to prepare?'

Rannveig thought of all they would have to do for a double wedding feast: the beasts to kill, bread to bake, new braid at least on her best apron-skirt. It would be a rush.

'Of course,' Manga said. 'Say yes, Ranka, and marry him quickly, or he'll change his mind and go off a-viking again.'

Saebjörn shook his head. 'I've had enough of roving. I want to settle down with a fine wife.'

She suspected it wasn't true. Come the spring the sea would call him... but for now he was home at last. 'Yes,' she said. Her hand reached for his; their fingers curled together. 'Let's be married at Winternights.'

Other titles by Marsali Taylor:

The Cass Lynch Mysteries

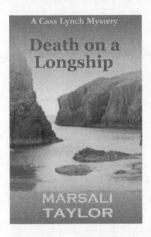

Death on a Longship

When she wangles the job of skippering a Viking longship for a film, Cass Lynch thinks her big break has finally arrived - even though it means returning home to the Shetland Islands, which she ran away from as a teenager. Then the 'accidents' begin - and when a dead woman turns up on the boat's deck, Cass realises that she, her family and her past are under suspicion from the disturbingly shrewd Detective Inspector Macrae. Cass must call on all her local knowledge, the wisdom she didn't realise she'd gained from sailing and her glamorous, French opera singer mother to clear them all of suspicion - and to catch the killer before Cass becomes the next victim.

Praise for *Death on a Longship:* ...You cannot go wrong with this delight of mystery! ... I love it when authors keep things current and relevant to today's issues as well as presenting us with a mystery to solve.
Mysteries etc

IBSN 987-1-78375-545-5

The Trowie Mound Murders

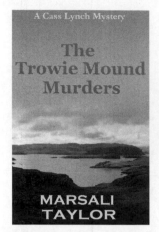

When a visiting yachting couple go missing from the Shetland oil capital of Brae, sailing skipper Cass Lynch overcomes her mistrust of the land world to ask for help from her old adversary DI Gavin Macrae. He discovers a link to international art theft, and warns Cass to steer clear – but when one of her sailing pupils goes missing, she goes alone to discover the secrets of the Neolithic tomb known locally as a 'trowie mound' ... Ghosts, folklore and a nail-biting finale at the local show come together to make an atmospheric, fast-moving thriller.

Praise for *The Trowie Mound Murders:* Shetland's landscape, sea ways, and history are integral to the plot as is its language (there's a handy glossary at the back for dialect words) which really gives a sense of the place. ... I'm really excited about the next book, it's going to be fun seeing what Cass does next.
Desperate Reader blogspot

IBSN 978-1-78375-513-4

A Handful of Ash

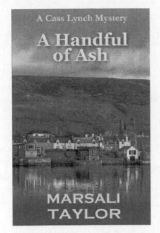

Liveaboard skipper Cass Lynch is busy with student life at the marine college in Shetland's ancient capital of Scalloway – until she finds a dead girl, whose hand is smeared with peat ash. Is this part of some strange ritual linking back to the witches once burned in Scalloway? What was the horned figure seen carrying the body? Rumours begin to spread, encouraged by local Hallowe'en traditions. Then there's a second murder ...

Praise for *A Handful of Ash*: I enjoyed this book enormously... the mystery itself held me enthralled. The suspects are numerous, and kept me guessing. When the murderer is revealed it was satisfying to see that the clues were all there for the amateur sleuth, provided you are a student of human nature. ... Highly recommended.

Lizzie Hayes, *Mystery People e-zine*

IBSN 978-1-78375-512-7

The Body in the Bracken

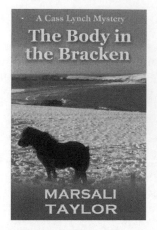

Cass Lynch has been persuaded to spend Christmas in the Highlands with her friend DI Gavin Macrae, but their romantic walk by the loch is cut short when they find a skeleton among the bracken. Back home in Shetland, Cass hears about Ivor Hughson, who left his wife and failed business months ago, and hasn't been heard of since. A near-disaster aboard Cass's yacht suggests someone wants to stop her asking questions about his disappearance. Meanwhile, there are eerie reports of sightings of a njuggle, a Shetland water-horse which drowns curious passers-by. Soon it's taking Cass all her wits to stay alive...

Praise for *The Body in the Bracken*: ... the real joy of Marsali Taylor's work is the richness of her portrayal of the Shetland background and inhabitants, and the effortless weaving in of Cass Lynch's sailing background, which is intrinsic to her personality and the USP of this growing series. ... Cass Lynch is an unusual protagonist, a stand-out in an overcrowded genre.'

Lynne Patrick, *Mystery People.*

IBSN: 978-1-78375-854-8

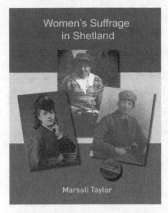

Women's Suffrage in Shetland

Only a small society in a remote group of islands ... yet Shetland had women on the school boards as early as London and Edinburgh. The first suffrage speakers came here in 1873; the first President of the 1909 Shetland Women's Suffrage Society marched with Mrs Pankhurst, and the second President was the wife of Asquith's Secretary for Scotland. Taylor takes the reader from the first calls of 'Votes for Women' in the French and American revolutions through the long struggle up to World War I – where many Shetland woman left the isles as nurses and canteen workers – and up to the vote at last.

Praise for *Women's Suffrage in Shetland.* Splendid ... an indication of how much more there can be done in the field of women's history in Shetland.
Angus Johnson, Archives Assistant, SMUA.

The Story of Busta House

Busta House was once owned by Shetland's most prosperous merchant, yet a family tragedy precipitated it into a ruinous court case which left the owner bankrupt, and his heirs dispossessed. This book tells the story of the house from the earliest records up to the present day, and ends with an account of the 'ghost of Busta'.

FORGOTTEN HEROINES
The diaries of Ysabel Birkbeck, Ambulance Driver on the Romanian Front, 1916-17, edited by Douglas Gordon Baxter and Marsali Taylor.

When Dr Elsie Inglis offered the War Office two front-line units staffed entirely by women, she was told to 'go home and sit still'. Her reply was to create the Scottish Women's Hospital for Foreign Service, funded through the National Union of Women's Suffrage Societies. Ysabel Birkbeck, author of these diaries, drove an ambulance for Inglis' last field hospital, attached to the First Serbian Division.

The drivers of *Forgotten Heroines* show how World War I was the turning-point in Edwardian women's emancipation. The Buffs, as they called themselves, were mostly 'surplus' county daughters who'd resigned themselves to a life of good works and flower arranging. This was the most interesting time they'd ever had, and they made the most of it. They cut their hair short, wore breeches, and were reproved by Dr Inglis for their swearing. There were balls and excursions between aeroplane bombardments, and they learned to flirt in French, German and Russian. While the army retreated, they continued to ferry the wounded from the front line; their Model T Fords were the last vehicles to cross the Danube. They inched through marshes by moonlight, and stuck in wheel-deep mud so often that all chauffeurs became known as 'shovers'. They were often hungry, ill, exhausted and afraid ... but the only time they were bored was when a male mechanic was sent from England to take over the cars they'd coaxed and fixed themselves for three months. Birkbeck's diaries show how their intelligence, endurance and courage were tested, and how they thrived on the challenge.

142

About Marsali Taylor: MARSALI TAYLOR grew up near Edinburgh, and came to Shetland in 1981 as a newly-qualified teacher of English, French and Drama. She is also a qualified STGA tourist-guide who is fascinated by history. She has published a number of plays in Shetland's distinctive dialect. She's a keen sailor who enjoys exploring in her own 8m yacht, and an active member of her local drama group. Her Shetland-set detective novels starring liveaboard sailor Cass Lynch have gained enthusiastic reviews both here and abroad, with the Shetland setting and characters getting particular praise.